ALSO BY RACHAEL HERRON

Cypress Hollow Yarns

Abigail's Shop

Lucy's Kiss

Naomi's Wish

Cora's Heart

Fiona's Flame

Eliza's Home

The Songbirds of Darling Bay

The Darling Songbirds

The Songbird's Call

The Songbird Sisters

The Firefighters of Darling Bay

Blaze

Burn

Flame

Heat

The Ballard Brothers of Darling Bay

On the Market

Build it Strong

Rock the Boat

Darling Bay Short Stories

A Darling Bay Christmas: Three Heartwarming Holiday Short
Stories

Honeymooning: A Cypress Hollow Yarn Short Story

Women's Fiction Novels

The Ones Who Matter Most

Splinters of Light

Pack Up the Moon

Memoir

A Life in Stitches: Knitting My Way Through Love, Loss, and
Laughter - Tenth Anniversary Edition

Unstuck: An Audacious Hunt for Home and Happiness

Nonfiction

Fast-Draft Your Memoir: Write Your Life Story in 45 Hours

Fast-Draft Your Memoir: The Workbook

Letters to New Authors: 29 Encouraging Letters to Your Inner
Writer

Thrillers (as R. H. Herron)

Stolen Things

Hush Little Baby

HEAT

THE FIREFIGHTERS OF DARLING BAY 4

RACHAEL HERRON

Hga

CONTENTS

Publisher's Note: This is a work of fiction. Names, characters, places, and incidents are a product of the author's imagination. Locales and public names are sometimes used for atmospheric purposes. Any resemblance to actual people, living or dead, or to businesses, companies, events, institutions, or locales is completely coincidental.

Heat / Rachael Herron. -- 2nd ed.
HGA Publishing
Copyright © 2014, Rachael Herron
All rights reserved.
ISBN-13: 978-1-940785-76-9

"It's a right turn, here." Bonnie pointed out the ambulance window. "At the post office."

Caswell Lloyd ignored her, blowing past the turn. The siren blared, and two children in a crosswalk waved.

"Caz?" Bonnie waved back at the kids and then blew out a breath, thumping backward into her seat. "Fine. If you think you know where you're going better than I do, even though you've worked this zone, for what, like five minutes?"

He didn't even have the grace to look her direction as he turned right at the bookstore.

Bonnie bit the inside of her mouth to keep from saying another word. They'd been on three calls so far that day, and he'd been like this on all of them, taciturn, practically non-verbal, and now he wasn't even driving in the right direction. He was going to have to double back half a block. Precious seconds would be lost, seconds that might mean the difference between life and death...

Well. Since they were responding to a medical alarm at

Ava Simon's house, the chances were pretty good it wasn't that big a deal. When Ava's grandkids had given her the medical pendant a year before, she'd spent the first two months pushing it just "to see how fast you could get here."

Bonnie hated change in her ambulance. Just when she'd finally gotten used to her partner, she'd gotten stuck with someone new. Johnny Kling, her last partner, had taken her six months to train, and then he'd been promoted to fire-fighter and transferred to Engine Three, moving Caz up the list to Station One. Of course, Johnny took the transfer. They all went somewhere—anywhere—to get off the ambo.

The problem lay in the fact that a lot of the guys, although they were all paramedics, didn't actually *want* to be on the ambulance. Ever. They wanted to do their para-medic time and mark it off their checklists. They wanted to hurry up and promote. Then they could do what they really wanted to do which was roll code three to the calls in their nice, clean engines, assess the patient, save a life with some simple CPR if they could, and then hand that patient over to Bonnie and whoever she was paired with for the difficult and stressful transport to the hospital—drives during which the recently-saved patient might code and have to be restarted all over again, while the vehicle flew fifty miles-per-hour around curves. It didn't help that the medics were the ones who spent hours waiting for busy hospital staff to take over care of patients, not the firefighters. The medics (not the firefighters) were the ones who ended up covered in vomit or worse. Who cleaned out the ambulance after a particularly gross call? Bonnie and her partner did.

The thing was, Bonnie freaking loved it. Maybe few others did, but she knew she belonged on the ambulance. She'd taken and passed all the classes, her log books were signed off. She could promote to firefighter during any testing phase. But she didn't want to. Riding in the back of the ambulance, pushing the morphine and then holding the hand of a person who was more scared than they'd ever been in their whole lives? Nothing was better than being the person who got to look a terrified patient in the eye and reassure them that yes, she was going to be just fine.

Even if it was—an awful lot of the time—a lie.

It was a lie Bonnie Maddern was honored to tell, a lie she believed every time she told it. Because if she didn't believe her patient was going to make it, who would?

Caz had figured out his mistake and made the correct turn.

"There," Bonnie said, gesturing to the old house. It was covered in peeling olive paint, and upstairs, a broken window was held together with blue painter's tape. A yellowed curtain hung crookedly at one window, and a rusted bicycle missing one wheel was upside down in what might have been a garden at one time.

Caz still hadn't said a word to her.

Fantastic.

Bonnie hadn't spent much time with Caz since he'd joined the department two years before. He'd been consistently assigned to a different house, and they'd only crossed on overtime shifts, never partnered. He'd always seemed a bit too cocksure, too confident, with that wide cowboy walk of his that took up too much of the hallway now that he was at Station One. It was too bad he was so good-looking, the rancher version of Matthew McConaughey. Caz's intensely light blue eyes made it startling to run into him in the dayroom. It made him a little less easy to ignore.

But heck. There was no rule they *had* to talk on the

ambulance, aside from what was necessary to the job. They didn't have to be friends. It was only ten days a month, she told herself. She could handle anything ten days a month, even a guy like Caz. Walking up the driveway in silence with him, Bonnie realized she was actually missing Jimmy's persistent throat-clearing.

Bonnie knocked on the door.

No answer.

Caz reached around her and knocked louder. Yeah, he probably thought he could even do that better than she could.

From inside, they heard a woman yell, "It's open!"

Inside, the house appeared somewhat clean. That was just about all it had going for it. The decades-old wallpaper —green and yellow stripes—was in as good repair as the peeling paint outside. The thin orange carpet at their feet must have been installed in the sixties or seventies. It smelled, as always, of garlic and lentils and something sweet, maybe a tropical air freshener.

In a tattered recliner sat Ava, an elderly woman who looked as if she'd been in place for as many years as the carpet. "Hello, hello!" Her curly white hair was tucked neatly behind her ears, and she wore three pairs of glasses— one on top of her head, one on her face, and one hung around her neck by a long blue plastic cord.

"Hiya," said Caz easily. Oh, so he *could* talk.

Bonnie came forward with her bag. "What's going on today, Mrs. Simon?" There was no television in the sparely furnished room, just a couch and a small red table with two matching wooden chairs. She wasn't holding a book, nor was there anything in her lap. Had she just been sitting there? For how long?

Caz reached forward, "Caswell Lloyd, ma'am. Pleasure to meet you. I'm new on the ambulance."

He was trying to charm her? He knew how?

"Ava Simon," the woman said. "So glad you've come. I wish I could offer you a cup of coffee, but I'm fresh out."

"Not to worry. I had my required pot before I left the station." He crouched in front of her, smiling. "What can we do for you today? How are you feeling?"

At least the man was a little less scary-looking when he smiled. He went from resembling the Matthew McConaughey of *True Detective* to the one in *Magic Mike*.

The woman's face brightened. "Oh, my. I'm just fine, thank you for asking, you big hunk of good-looking, you."

Bonnie stepped forward. "All righty. Let's get a read on your blood pressure. Did you take your medicine today?"

Ava frowned at her and pushed away the BP cuff. Sitting forward, she peered around Bonnie and smiled at Caz. "Caswell Lloyd, you said? Any relation to Harrison Lloyd?"

"My grandfather, ma'am."

"Oh," said Ava with a giggle. "I had such a crush on him years ago, when we attended the same church. Such a fine man he was. And handsome! Just like you. You got your blue eyes from him, eh?"

"Thank you kindly, ma'am. Now. What's the problem today?"

Ava batted her lashes at Caz. "It's my toilet, honey. Something's just not right."

"Your toilet?" sputtered Bonnie. "That's why you pushed your alarm? Okay, that's just not—"

Caz cut her off. "I'm sure Bonnie won't mind giving that a quick look while I look at something a little prettier. Mind if I take your pulse?"

Bonnie stomped down the hall. The guy had *nerve*.

Plumbing was the worst. There was a reason she didn't work the truck with its water removal tools. She hated the way water glugged through a clogged pipe and she literally had to call a plumber to get the hair out of her own bath drain—the look of a sodden clump of gunk being pulled out was enough to make her gag.

Working on someone else's toilet *really* wasn't what she'd gone into the fire profession to do.

But it was better than watching Caz Lloyd flirt with Ava Simon. How was she going to work a whole *year* with him?

Five minutes later, after quite a bit of plunging accompanied by increasingly creative under-her-breath cursing, the toilet was almost clear. She could hear Caz and Ava laughing.

Oh, good. They were having a fine time while she used brute force and listened to pipes gurgle angrily.

"I'm doing fine! Thanks for asking!" Bonnie blew her short blond hair out of her eyes. She gave one final shove of the plunger, but she did such a fine job of it that she couldn't pull it back out again. She put one foot against the toilet and pulled harder. "Dang it, do *not* tick me off, you old porcelain bucket, you." One more pull.

With a small scream, Bonnie toppled backward as the toilet came off its seal, pulling away from the wall. There was a crash as the porcelain bowl and tank smashed into a thousand pieces, followed by a flood of dirty water that covered her from the waist down. The brown water was quickly followed by a frigid high-pressure spray of clean water, which jetted out of the pipe in the wall, hitting her in the face.

From the living room she heard Caz roar, "What's going on in there?"

"Don't worry!" she yelled back. "I've got this!" Then she drummed her legs against the floor in a quick wordless fit, took a moment set her lips into a determined and very firmly closed line. Then she lunged at the pipe.

CHAPTER 2

I t was Caz's turn to cook, his first night at Station One.
Seeing as he'd already gotten crap from two of the guys
for browning the meat too well on the industrial stove's
huge burners, it wasn't going great so far. Not that he cared
that much. He wasn't here to make friends, after all.

Tox Ellis, the engine's captain, leaned over his shoulder.
"That's too many onions. Coin is gonna throw a fit."

Caz didn't respond. It was usually the best course of
action, he'd found.

"You gonna take some out or what?"

Did the guy actually think he was going to redo dinner
because of someone's preference? "No."

"Coin *really* hates onions."

"Then I guess he can make his own damn dinner."

Tox grunted. "You came from Los Robles FD, right?"

Caz nodded. Was he going to have to talk right up until
the food was on the table? Was that a requirement here?
The way Bonnie Maddern chattered on the ambulance, it
might well be.

"You worked with John Martini?"

He nodded again. Hopefully, the guy would get the hint. He didn't want to be out and out rude—next to the battalion chief, it was clear that Tox ruled the roost around this station. It wouldn't do to get on his bad side. But when Caz cooked, he liked doing it in silence.

Heck, he liked doing just about everything in silence. He thought of Bonnie again. Never quiet, except after that last run when she'd been covered in toilet water.

Tox popped a piece of red pepper in his mouth.

Caz *hated* it when people messed with his cooking. "Do you mind?"

The man's thick eyebrows rose? "Not really. I like peppers. You got plenty. So, you and Martini get along?"

Martini had been a blowhard engineer with britches that were about a mile too big for his five-foot-nothing frame. It was better not to answer. "Is anyone going to mind garlic?"

"Nah. What about Horton, is he still a battalion chief there?"

"Yeah."

"Good guy, huh?"

Horton was one of the most boring people he'd ever met in his life. But he wasn't bad. "I guess."

"You're a tough nut, huh?"

"Look, I just want to cook these carnitas and get it over with. That okay with you?"

"What's your problem?" Tox's voice didn't seem to carry the normal venom that went with those words. He seemed honestly curious. And no way was Caz going to confide in him.

"Hand me the cayenne?"

Tox sighed and gave over the Costco-sized container. "Whatever. You don't have to have friends here, man, but a forty-eight hour shift is long. It goes easier if you play well with others."

"I hear you."

"There anything else you want to say?"

Caz stopped and looked directly at the man. "I have no idea what you want from me."

"Man," said Tox, clearly at the end of his friendly tolerance. He'd lasted longer than most. "How about chill the freak out?" He stalked out of the kitchen.

Caz focused on the blade of his knife. Pineapple, instead of making the meat sweet, tenderized it. And it was satisfying to chop. He thunked off the top and the bottom, then whacked at the sides of it.

"What's that?" His next kitchen intruder was the tall engineer named Hank Coffee. He seemed nice enough, more mellow than Tox, but he was part of the house's noise and bluster, too.

"A pineapple," said Caz simply.

"I'm allergic."

"Okay." He didn't stop chopping.

"Are you really going to put that in dinner?"

"Yes."

"Even though I told you I'm allergic?"

Caz's knife slowed and he looked up. "I figured Tox told you to say that. Are you really?"

Hank blinked. "No."

"Okay, then."

Hank leaned against the counter easily, as if he had nowhere better to be. "So tell me about yourself."

Caz hated open-ended questions that weren't really even questions at all. "Nothing much to tell."

"You married?"

He also hated yes or no questions. "Nope."

"Kids?"

"Nope." Caz finished chopping the pineapple and dumped it into the pork shoulder on the stove.

"You live nearby?"

"Nope."

"Dude. You make it hard to talk to you, anyone ever tell you that?"

"Heard it said."

Hank didn't give up, though. "Okay, then, where do you live? Exactly?"

Maybe if Caz answered a couple of questions, he'd go away. "About fifteen miles outside town, due east out 119."

"There's nothing out there."

Well, on one hand that was true, there was a whole lot of nothing near Caz's ranch. But that was the best part of it. Nothing and no one. "We raise horses. My dad does." *Did.*

"Well, that's something." Hank looked cheered. "You're a cowboy. That explains the hat in your truck."

"What were you doing looking in my truck?"

"I was snooping," said Hank cheerfully. "I do that. Who takes care of your horses while you're at work?"

"My foreman."

"Fancy! You got a foreman! Is it a dude ranch? Can I come out and ride?"

"No."

"Why not?" Just like Tox, Hank seemed curiously friendly.

And Caz was tired of avoiding the question. "I don't like people very much."

"Firefighters? Citizens? Men? Women? *All* people?"

Caz slid the pre-chopped onions into the pot and turned the heat to high. "Pretty much all of 'em."

"Yeah, see, I don't believe that."

"You should."

"Nah," said Hank. "I talked to your field training officer, Bert."

Caz's FTO at Los Robles FD had been a man who never, ever, *ever* shut up. "Huh."

"Yeah. And he said that when it comes to patient care, you're right up there with the best he's seen."

Caz just added more cayenne. Maybe he could burn his new coworkers' chit-chat buds right off.

"And what I think is that goes directly against what I've seen from you in this house. You don't talk, you don't smile, you don't laugh. But Bert says you make people feel safe. And that's not a thing that someone who doesn't like people does." Hank paused as if he thought Caz might say something. When he didn't speak, Hank went on, "So that makes me feel better, at least, because you're kind of acting like a tool around here. I'm willing to put that down to nerves."

That's not what it was. Not at all. Caz added a healthy dose of cumin to the pot.

"Do you even want to be here?" Hank's voice was tighter now.

"I do." That was the simplest answer to a complex question.

"Did you like your last department?"

"Not really."

"Why did you leave?"

Caz sighed. "I didn't get along with staff."

"Surprise, surprise. Do you like it here better, so far?"

"No." Especially not if he was going to have to put up with Bonnie Maddern as a partner for the next year. How was he supposed to ignore someone as pretty and *pushy* as she was? But what could he do? It seemed like the woman could talk the hind leg off a donkey, and probably would if given half a chance. It didn't help that she was so dang pretty sometimes he forgot to mind that she was talking. Her short blond bob was always a little uneven, as if she'd woken up and just run her fingers through it to smooth it—yeah, her hair bothered Caz, mostly because he found his fingers itching to see if it felt as soft as it looked.

He hadn't taken the Darling Bay job in order to meet a woman, though.

Paying for his father's care was why Caz had applied for and accepted the higher-paying job, even as far away from his cabin as it was.

Caz knew himself. He could put up with just about anything. They could pair him up with Tox (talk about someone who *never* shut up) or make him clean the bathrooms every day. He was the FNG, after all, the freaking new guy. Caz just wanted to come to work, do his job, collect his paycheck, and go home. That surely couldn't be too much to ask.

Hank laughed. "So you seriously don't like being here? Jeez. Why stay then?"

"Because I think it's a good department. I think I can learn to like it. Or at least tolerate it."

"You always this dang honest?"

"Yes."

"Why not just stay on your ranch and raise horses?"

"Not enough money in it." That was the sad truth. For Dad's full-time care, Caz needed a full-time job. That was the bitter catch-22.

Hank's eyes were bright. He was enjoying this give and take, even if Caz wasn't. "Do you like *horses*, at least?"

"Not really." Caz was a woodworker, not a horse man. But where did these guys get the idea that you got to like what you did for a living?

"You are a cranky sum-gun, ain'tcha?"

"I've heard that on occasion, too."

Hank rapped his empty plastic cup against the counter firmly. "Well. I'll let you alone, then."

Finally.

"But I gotta say one thing. There're good men in this department. Good women, too, just outnumbered. You got one riding in your ambulance with you. There's no reason you can't make friends here. But you gotta want to."

Caz knew that. He turned up the heat again and poked the meat with a wooden spoon.

He heard the kitchen door swing shut behind Hank. Alone again.

Good.

CHAPTER 3

The nice thing about the women's bathroom at Station One, the thing that the men's didn't have, was a glazed window in the shower. It was always closed for safety, of course. You wouldn't want a random drunk citizen hauling himself in and roaming the station halls in the middle of the night. But when Bonnie was in the shower, there was no harm in her sliding the window open. Like a dog propping a chin on a car windowsill, Bonnie rested her chin on the tiled ledge, resting her eyes on the long swathe of green grass behind the station. It was marred a little by the big concrete driveway that ran through the apparatus bay, but that was a necessary evil. On the other side of the drive was a stand of eucalyptus trees that went right down to the creek that was still rushing with the March rains. Around dinner time, the frogs who lived on its banks started their deafening chorus. The wild California poppies that dotted their edges of the station lawn had shut for the night even though twilight hadn't fully settled.

It was her favorite time of night. And this was her

favorite thing to do—to stand in the hot shower, watching the quiet riverbank. At any moment, the tones could go off in the station, and four minutes later—still damp under her hastily-thrown-on uniform—she might be on the road, bouncing up and down in the tech seat, racing for whatever disaster (or stubbed toe) had prompted one of the Darling Bay citizens to dial 911. But the tones stayed blessedly quiet. The frogs chirruped. A soft breeze sighed in the tall eucalyptus, and Bonnie, her body and hair newly sewage-free, closed her eyes in happiness.

This was, truly, the life. She couldn't be any luckier. She heard her mother's voice in her head, "Everything is good when you look at it from the right direction." Heck, even getting doused by disgusting toilet water meant that she got to hang out in the shower at a time when she wasn't keeping any of the other women in the station from taking theirs. All the other women in the station, of course, were dispatchers, since Bonnie was the only female firefighter on A shift. The dispatchers tended to take their showers as soon as they woke up in the morning, and since their hours were more tightly scheduled, Bonnie tried to stay out of their way as much as possible.

The water beating against her back was gloriously hot. She redirected it so that it hit more of her as she turned so she could rest her cheek against the window's ledge. The cool air of the spring night blew on the crown of her wet hair. She kept her eyes closed and sighed in pleasure.

The breeze got stronger. Huh. Warmer, too. She waited for the evening air to shift, but instead, she smelled mint.

Mint gum. Spearmint, to be exact. Like someone was standing outside blowing on her head.

She opened her eyes and jerked her head upright, but

she didn't quite avoid the light slap aimed at her cheek. Tox, standing outside in the flower border, roared with laughter. She slammed the window shut and yelled through it, "You jacknut! I could have died! I could have slipped and *died* and then you'd be back on the ambulance and you'd be *so sorry!*"

Bonnie heard more male laughter join Tox's. She sighed. At least there was no way he could have peeked in downward. The worst he'd seen was the top of her wet head. Good thing, too. If he'd seen more, Bonnie would have cheerfully called his girlfriend Grace from the day room so everyone could listen, and she would have taken great pleasure in telling Grace what her big dumb captain boyfriend had done. Bonnie pulled down her towel and dried herself.

Idiot boys. It was like living with eight big brothers.

She pulled on her uniform roughly, not caring the backs of her knees and spine weren't totally dry. Speed was important while getting dressed at the station. She'd been tempting fate wasting time in the shower anyway.

The six o'clock tone buzzed overhead, and over the intercom, Tox yelled, "Dinner! Dinner time."

Bonnie checked with dispatch before going down to the kitchen. Only Lexie was working, Sue must have already been in the dorm on her sleep shift. "You eating with us tonight?"

Lexie looked over her computer screen, her red curls crazily piled on her head, her smile bright. "Nope! I'm good!"

"Dang, you're cheerful. What's up with you?" Bonnie tapped the tiny firefighter wind chime that dangled next to Lexie's terminal, making it tinkle softly.

"Um..."

From the floor behind Lexie's terminal, Coin Keefe said, "Hiya." He was lying on the floor on his back, next to Lexie's chair.

"Holy—" What had she interrupted? "Get a room, you two!"

"It's not what it looks like," said Coin.

Bonnie looked at Lexie for an answer, but she was giggling too hard to answer.

Slowly, Coin sat up. "You know I got that neck pain." He pointed to the pillow he'd been lying on. It was covered with tiny plastic spikes.

"Oh, no," said Bonnie, backing up, her hands in front of her. "Seriously. If that's some kind of kink, I so don't need to know. At *all*. Private lives should be kept that way..."

Lexie laughed harder and then finally choked out, "It's an acupressure pillow. Grace gave it to me when my neck was bothering me, and it's been helping Coin. He just didn't want y'all down the hall to know."

Bonnie raised an eyebrow. "So that's the only reason he's hiding out of sight behind your work station?"

Blushing, Lexie nodded. Coin, never the most outgoing of Bonnie's shift mates, said, "And that's my cute. Dang. I mean my cue..." He hurriedly dropped a kiss on Lexie head and raced out of dispatch.

Lexie, finally bringing herself under control, said, "He's ridiculous. I have no idea why I put up with him."

Bonnie sank into a chair. "You're crazy about him."

Lexie ducked her head. "Anyway. What's up? Why aren't you eating?"

"I'm going to. Wanted to see if you wanted anything."

"Nah." Lexie waved a hand at a plate of rice and beans on her terminal. "I've been picking at this for hours. I'm fine."

"Cold food isn't the same as fresh, warm stuff."

"Dispatchers are used to cold food." 911 rang. Lexie reached for the button and said, "Speaking of which..." While she questioned the caller over her headset, she dispatched Engine Three and Medic Five using her foot pedal.

"No, ma'am, don't slap him on the back. That could push the marble farther into his windpipe. Just keep him still." She gave a kind laugh. "I know, it's hard with a three-year-old to keep him from climbing around. I know you're doing a great job. I'll just keep you on the line till the first unit pulls up, okay? You let me know when you hear the siren."

Without asking, Bonnie picked up Lexie's plate, added a sprinkle more of cheese on top, and zapped it in the microwave. By the time the engine was on scene and Lexie had hung up, her food was warm again.

"You didn't need to do that."

"I know," said Bonnie. "But you're just so *stuck* in this cage."

"Hey, I like my cage. It fits me."

Bonnie rubbed the edge of the round table. It was slightly sticky, and that, unlike Lexie's food temperature, was none of her business. She had to spend enough time cleaning the kitchen and day room with the rest of the guys —she didn't need to clean in here, too. "Your cage doesn't get to roll lights-and-sirens to anything."

"My cage doesn't need to be mopped down for blood."

Bonnie pointed at the stickiness on the table. "For germs, though."

"Dang it," said Lexie. "I *told* Sue she had to clean up after using her dang pressure cooker, but she never listens."

The firehouse was a family. And it was a nice thing, of

course. The camaraderie that automatically came with the job was something Bonnie loved. What most people didn't know, though, was how dysfunctionally family-like fire-houses could be. It wasn't funny or cute when one captain refused to *ever* rinse a plate before sticking it in the rather mediocre dishwasher. When PeeWee left the house's groceries on the counter for six hours because he didn't "feel" like putting them in the fridge, and three of them got sick on the pork as a result, they weren't grateful PeeWee was a fire brother. No, just like any other brother who screwed up, the firefighters had hated his guts for a good week. He'd had to clean the station bathrooms for a month in penance, and that was no small punishment.

Lexie got out a wet wipe to scrub at the spot.

"Later," said Bonnie. "Eat your food, lady. Before you fall over from hunger."

Lexie patted her not-very-thin waistline. With her bright red hair and lips and her blue uniform, she looked a little like a pinup girl stuck in the wrong clothes. "Do I look like I'm suffering? If Coin and his daughter don't quit making me those caramel turtle cookies, I'm going to need to get a new pair of uniform pants, stat."

"Yeah, I think Coin likes you just fine the way you are."

Lexie grinned and reached for her plate. "Yeah, I guess. He likes a girl with handles. And hey, I like the way he handles me. Oh, how did that last call go? Why did you have to return for cleanup if you didn't even transport the patient?"

Bonnie groaned. "It's what's-his-name's fault."

"The new guy? Caz..." Lexie scrabbled for her Telestaff roster. "Caswell Lloyd, that's it. I've only met him once. He's your new partner, right?"

Sighing, Bonnie said, "Yeah. Because he was too busy flirting with old Mrs. Simon, I had to deal with why she pushed her medical alert."

"Which was…"

"Her toilet."

"Oh, no."

"Oh, yes."

"She's been getting pretty bad lately. I worked overtime the other day on C shift and I took a call from the alarm company. She pushed the button because she couldn't get her beer open."

"You're *kidding.*"

"I sent one of the rounds guys instead of a full engine, but apparently she yelled at him after he dropped the beer —it was her only bottle— and he came back looking pretty pale. I felt kind of bad for him. So you had to, what? Plunge a backup?" Lexie snorted.

"I wish. That's how it started, but it turned out that while they were out in the living room yukking it up, I might have been a little too…emphatic in my plunging."

"Mmm?" Lexie folded in her lips and her eyes danced.

"I yanked the whole thing off its seal because of the slant of her old crooked floor, and the whole thing tipped over. It crashed."

"As in broke?" Lexie covered her mouth.

"As in shattered. I was covered in—"

Lexie held up a hand. "I'm eating."

"You can eat through anything! I've seen you drink a milkshake while listening to a guy vomit in your ear."

"That's different. That's far away." Lexie wrinkled her nose in Bonnie's direction. "You, you're closer. You were covered in…poop. And then you put *cheese* on my *plate.*"

"I took a shower! A long one! New clothes!"

"Hmmm." Lexie appeared to be considering whether or not to let her stay. "I suppose…"

Bonnie stood. "Fine, I have to eat dinner anyway."

"Wait, wait. What did you do?"

"What could I do? That's why we were out of service so long. I had to clean and disinfect her whole bathroom and remove the rubble. Then we went to the hardware store, where I bought her a new toilet."

"Your own money?"

"Can you even imagine what Susie Costello would do if I turned it in for reimbursement? She'd deny it so fast she'd get a nosebleed."

Lexie laughed.

Bonnie glared. "You're not being very helpful for someone who says she's in the helping business."

"You put it in? Yourself?"

Straightening her shoulders, Bonnie nodded. "Turns out I'm good with plumbing. Even though I *hate* it. I even added one of those fancy new seat-warmer bidets."

"Holy crap. Pun intended."

Bonnie couldn't help smiling. Mrs. Simon had really liked the idea of it, giving her a smile that had up till that point been reserved for Caz. And pleasing her had been the goal. If it kept Mrs. Simon from filing a complaint, then Bonnie didn't mind the couple hundred bucks she'd dropped to do it.

No, what she minded was the way Caz Lloyd had handled himself on the call. "So you're saying you don't know anything about the new guy?"

Lexie shook her head. "Just that he lateraled in from a department up north. Los Robles, maybe? I can't remember. People say he's pretty quiet."

Not with Mrs. Simon, he hadn't been. He'd been all charm, as if the old woman had tapped his side for maple syrup. But in the rig on the way to the hardware store, he'd just stared straight ahead as he drove. His only change of facial expression had been when he'd rolled down his window and the airflow wafted her stench over him. "Noxious," he'd muttered.

Bonnie had been too irritated to say anything at all.

"Caz helped you install the toilet, though, didn't he?" Lexie's eyes sparkled.

"You're loving this, aren't you?"

The dispatcher nodded. "Best story I've heard all day."

"No, he did *not*. And I hate him for it." Any other of her coworkers would have been in the bathroom with her, manhandling the pipes and telling her she was doing it wrong but helping anyway. "What he did was sit in Mrs. Simon's kitchen while she made him—and I'm not making this up—fresh peanut butter cookies. Meanwhile, I installed a new toilet, hooked up an electric bidet, and sanitized a room that was disgusting even before I dumped dirty toilet water all over it."

"Did you get a cookie?"

Bonnie's face burned. "I asked for one."

"They denied you?"

"He said I should clean up first or risk giving myself a disease."

"Did he bring one back for you?"

"You know he didn't."

Lexie said, "All right. He's on my to-be-woken-at-one-a.m. list."

Bonnie nodded in satisfaction. "That's all I'm asking. Hey! No, wait. I'm his partner! If you wake him, you wake me."

"Just enjoy his pain, my friend." Lexie gave her patented grin and Bonnie was grateful all over again to have the job she did. There was nothing better than working with friends.

She'd just *make* Caz become one. Whether he liked it or not.

CHAPTER 4

Bonnie tried for the next few medical runs to make Caz laugh. The first was at one a.m., just as Lexie had promised (not that Lexie had anything to do with it, she knew that, but it was satisfying to see Caz's sleep-creased face frowning in the dim light of the darkened apparatus bay). That was an easy run, a kid with asthma who was having difficulty breathing because she'd lost her inhaler. One hit of the nebulizer had stabilized her and they rolled code two to the hospital. Bonnie had told the little girl all her best jokes. (What's brown and sticky? A stick!) When she'd run out, she'd raised her voice to say, "Hey, Caz, what's your favorite joke?"

He'd ignored her.

"Hey! Buddy! You hear me?"

"I'm trying to drive here," was all he said.

"Yeah," she muttered with a cheeky grin at the girl. "Apparently he can only do one thing at a time. Me, I can take your blood pressure while I blow up this balloon."

"That's not a balloon!" the little girl said. "That's a plastic glove!"

Bonnie pretended surprise. "Oh, my gosh! I thought it was a turkey! Look! Here are all his feathers... Let's draw a face, huh? Here, use this pen."

Caz didn't even bother to glance over his shoulder at their awesome bird.

The next medical wasn't until eleven the next morning. The call was an elderly male with chest pain, and it was Caz's turn to be primary care while she drove but he remained tight-lipped through that run, too.

No, she took that back. He'd only been tight-lipped with *her*. Bonnie could admit that. Mr. Schmidt had been grumpy as sin when they got there, annoyed that his wife had called, annoyed that they were cluttering up his view of the television with their gear and bags.

Caz had kneeled next to the man's armchair and said something Bonnie couldn't hear. As if the sun had come from behind a cloud, Mr. Schmidt's face had creased into a blindingly-bright smile. "She is," he said to Caz. "She really is. Love of my life, that woman."

Mrs. Schmidt snapped, "Then let them put that heart machine thingie on you already."

"Fine, lovey." Mr. Schmidt looked up at Caz. "Do what you gotta do, son. You're right. I'd do anything for her."

Later, on their way back to quarters, Bonnie asked, "What did you say to him?"

"Why do you whistle so much?"

Startled, Bonnie said, "What? I wasn't whistling."

"You whistle all the *time*. It's like a nervous tic or something."

Funny, at the station, Tox had mentioned it recently also. It had pleased her, actually. Her grandmother had been a whistler. Gramma Honor had whistled when she was happy, which was most of the time, and when she was sad. Almost tuneless, it had been the background music of Bonnie's childhood. Sometimes she caught her mother doing it, too. "Huh. Was I doing it right now?"

"When you drive, you always whistle." He paused. "It's pretty annoying."

"Get over it," said Bonnie cheerfully, too pleased about by finding out she whistled like Gramma Honor to be bothered by his comment. "Back to my question. What did you say to him?"

"Who?" Caz was staring at his phone while she drove. He didn't even glance at her.

"Mr. Schmidt. How did you get him to go along with what we wanted him to do?"

"Nothing." He sounded put out to be asked.

Bonnie braked a little too hard at the red light at Bridge Road, and Caz jerked against his seatbelt. "You said something. Spill it."

"No."

Bonnie puffed out her breath. "Are you always this big a pain?"

He appeared to consider the question. Then he said, "Yes."

"Awesome."

"Are you always this talkative?"

Anger tingled at the ends of Bonnie's fingertips. She wrapped her hands tighter around the wheel. "You bet I am." She turned left into the shopping center.

"I thought we were heading to quarters."

"We were. Now we're getting ice cream."

"I made a sandwich for lunch."

Of course he had. It was probably the most boring sandwich ever made. "Let me guess," she said. "Bologna. Dry."

He frowned. "No."

"Peanut butter and really old jelly, the kind that's been on the door of your refrigerator for at least a year. On stale white bread."

He frowned harder. "No."

Bonnie smiled. At least a frown was a reaction. He was talking to her, no matter how minimally. "Liverwurst."

Caz couldn't hide the snort. "No."

"I can guess all day if you don't want to tell me."

"I'm torn."

"Between?"

"Between letting you guess all day and telling you the answer just to shut you up."

"Oh, go on and tell me. It'll tell me something about your character."

He looked out the window as if there was something interesting to be seen instead of just the pink and white awning over the taffy store. "Ham and cheese."

"On rye?"

"I have no idea."

Honestly exasperated, Bonnie blew out a breath. "How can you not know? Did your mommy make it for you?"

"Nope. But I did make the same kind for my dad before I left the ranch." The words came slowly from him, as if pulled from his throat one by one.

Pulling into the parking spot in front of the newly rebuilt Skip's Ice Cream, Bonnie hit the brakes too hard again and Caz rocked forward and back.

"Do you mind? I'd like to avoid whiplash."

"You live with your father?"

Caz gave her a look as black as new asphalt. "If you're getting ice cream, go get it."

"Oh, *you're* getting ice cream, too."

He crossed his arms. "I'll wait here. Leave the keys."

"So you can take off, leaving my sorry butt here?"

"I would never leave my partner."

"At least you have a few morals. Now, get out of the rig, or I'm going to get you a triple scoop of spumoni."

His scowl continued, but there was a glint of humor she'd never seen behind his blue eyes. "I love spumoni."

"No one loves spumoni."

Caz was finally beginning to reach for his door handle when the radio beeped. Lexie's voice said, "Engine One, Medic One, medical emergency, 378 Ritchie Street."

Bonnie sighed. "Saved by the bell." She put the ambulance in reverse. She wanted desperately to know why he lived with his father. He didn't seem like a family guy.

He seemed the opposite, more like he'd been raised by wolves.

CHAPTER 5

It wasn't a secret Caswell Lloyd had taken the job because of Battalion Chief Jack Barger. Barger's family had the adjoining property to the Lloyd's, and their families had been friends for almost a hundred years if you went back far enough. There was a rumor that a Lloyd had prevented a Barger from getting shot in the back in a bar once, but since that Barger got shot in the front a little later, some of the rumor couldn't quite be trusted.

But when it came down to trust, Caz knew one thing: he could trust the chief.

Until just about two minutes ago.

He stared at Barger. Usually when Barger was joking, his mustache wiggled up and down—it had been his tell for years and years. The mustache was still now.

"We have to what?"

Barger winced. "Did I stutter?"

Next to Caz, Bonnie seemed shocked into silence.

Chief Barger pinched the bridge of his nose and shut his eyes for a moment. "I don't want to run a charity fundraiser either, but the city manager has left me no wiggle room.

The Darling Bay Alzheimer's Support Initiative needs help keeping their doors open, and if we don't do it, I don't know who will. You of all people should understand that, Caz."

Him? The chief was going to bring his *father* into this?

"But," said Bonnie slowly. "There are charities who specialize in getting grants for that type of thing, aren't there?"

Chief Barger humphed. "*We* are the charity this time."

Bonnie clapped her hands against her thighs, as if she were calling Methyl, the station dog. "Okay, then! If we have to do this, we'll do it right."

Caz hated when the fire department was used as a wishing well. In his world, when people needed something, they went out and got it. They knew where to go to get it, and if they didn't, they found out. When his father had gotten to the point of needing a full-time caretaker, Caz had found one for him. He'd taken a week of vacation to do the interviews. He'd met with references. He'd treated it like his full-time job because it was that important. And when he needed more money, when his father's insurance refused to cover the meds he needed, Caz had changed jobs. Darling Bay was a sight smaller and a lot more provincial than his last agency, but they had funds. It was a tourist town. They paid their firefighters better than almost anyone else in the state.

Caz had left his cabin and his dream of finishing it, by hand the way he wanted to, behind him in his rearview mirror when he'd pointed the front of his truck at his new life.

That was the point. *You did what you needed to do, you didn't go looking for a handout.* He could feel his lips forming around the words, but Bonnie, as if reading his mind, kicked his shoe.

He changed the words to simply, "Why us?" Then he felt another swift kick to his ankle. "Hey!"

"Oh, my gosh, did I kick you? So sorry about that," Bonnie said sweetly. "Like I was saying, we'd be happy to help, Chief. What do you need?"

She was lying. No way did she want to do this any more than he did.

The chief nodded, apparently mollified. "The dinner has already been set up, and you should be grateful. Lexie and Coin got it donated from Caprese, and that was the hardest part. Hank and his girlfriend Samantha volunteered —" he looked over his glasses as if to imply *they* should be volunteering, too, "—to do the decorating of the apparatus bay. You'll both be in charge of the after-dinner fundraising." He pulled out a yellow legal pad. "We'll need some kind of entertainment. We need to get our citizens inside the apparatus bay and keep them there until they write a check big enough to leave. We'll have plenty of donated wine from Forget-Me-Not, so that'll help."

Bonnie looked at the paper. "So we have the venue and the drinks—we just need party games. Easy," she said brightly. "We've got this."

"But why—" Caz started.

Bonnie nudged his shoulder with hers. "Come on, buddy."

He wasn't her buddy. In truth, the chief was his only friend at the department. "Why us?"

Chief Barger leaned back, as if he'd been waiting for this. He flipped a yellow mechanical pencil from hand to hand. "You're the newest."

"I am," said Caz. "But she's not."

"Unluckily for her in this matter, you're her partner."

"But—"

"And I've heard that you two have been fighting."

Fighting? Fighting was when you had to haul a three hundred fifty pound man high on meth off his girlfriend who already had a broken nose. What he and Bonnie had been doing was squabbling, that was all. Nothing more. "Nah," Caz said.

"Fighting?" Bonnie shot him a look like she thought he'd ratted them out. "Really?"

"We're good, boss." The sooner they got out of here the sooner he could go back to the dayroom and work on the tiny horse he was whittling out of a scrap piece of oak.

"Best friends," said Bonnie. "Couldn't be closer."

Completely unbidden, an image of Bonnie being closer to him filled Caz's mind. Her lips, close to his. The scent of her—he caught it from here, light and flowery and somehow complex—filling his senses. His hand cupping her chin... The sudden image was unexpected and unwelcome and entirely way too hot. "Yep," he said, almost forgetting what he was agreeing to.

"You haven't been fighting over who's primary on calls?"

"Sure," said Bonnie easily. "Everyone argues over that."

"It's not really arguing," said Caz, even though it had gotten heated more than once already. The problem was that she thought she was better at patient care than he was. Just because he didn't want to talk to *her* (or any of the rest of the crew at the station, for that matter) didn't mean that he didn't want to talk to patients. He was good at it—he knew that. And she was a good driver. It was a match made in paramedic heaven.

Chief Barger leaned back in his chair and stared. "I heard you. You were shouting at each other like four-year-olds angry about whose turn it was to play with the toy truck."

Bonnie cleared her throat. Caz shifted uncomfortably in his chair.

They had, actually, been shouting at each other. They'd gotten a rash of crap about it later from the guys when they came back to quarters, too. Tox had said they sounded like cats fighting and Hank had said he'd almost called the cops to separate them. Caz had ignored them and Bonnie had said something funny that had defused the tension, but it had been nothing but embarrassing.

"Most partners take turns," said the chief. "Why the heck can't you just do that?"

They did. For the most part. The argument he'd overheard had been the first call of the last tour. Caz thought he should be primary because she'd been primary on the last call of their previous shift, and she'd thought they'd established that *she* was primary on the first call of a new shift.

"It was stupid of us," said Caz. "We apologize."

Bonnie nodded. "Now we roshambo for it. We're very sorry."

Chief Barger's mustache twitched. "You know what pisses me off the most about this?"

Caz could imagine, but he wasn't going to volunteer extra information.

"Let me tell you," the chief went on. "Let me *illuminate* you. You wasted time. Have I ever told you how I feel about wasted time in this department?"

Caz had only been a member of the department for a few months and he'd heard it more than a couple of times already. But you couldn't tell Jack that.

"Wasted time means you're *killing* someone."

Caz and Bonnie met eyes. Her lips were pulled in as if she were putting on lipstick, her brown eyes wide. He could feel the muscle in his forehead jump, the one that always twitched when he clenched his teeth.

The chief put both hands flat on the table in front of him. "You're in *my* apparatus bay yelling at each other? Every second you're doing that after dispatch is a second you're sending someone into an early grave. Seconds mean lives saved. You think that little boy at the bottom of the pool cares which one of you is primary? You think the old guy who just coded gives a crap who's a better driver? Your *egos* are the only things you're saving when you're fighting like an old married couple. There's no way I'm going to tolerate that in *my* house. You hear me?"

A man with less experience might mention that on the day in question they'd been dispatched to a thirty-year-old who'd tripped and sprained her ankle in front of her own house. No one had been dying. Caz caught Bonnie's eye again. Something flipped low in his stomach. He'd call it relief that she wasn't going to argue with the chief, either. That wasn't what it was, though. It was something more primal than just simple relief.

"We hear you, Chief," said Caz simply.

"Totally," said Bonnie. "We're very sorry. It won't happen again." She blinked and Caz had to tear his eyes from her mouth, which was puckered into something that was probably concern but actually looked highly kissable, which wasn't an appropriate thought to have about his partner, ever, especially not at that moment.

Chief Barger nodded and looked satisfied. "Good. Raise the money they need, or we'll have this same conversation at a louder volume next time. Now get out of my office."

CHAPTER 6

"Don't put that there, honey." Bonnie's mother Marge flapped her hands. She took the fat white candle out of Bonnie's hands and set it on a low glass table. "Oh, sugar, you really are a bull in a china shop, aren't you?"

Bonnie couldn't count the number of times she'd heard that in her life. Her mother *owned* the china shop (okay, it was an antique shop, Darling Trinkets, sandwiched between the pizza shop and the bike rental place), and Bonnie had always been the bull. "I just wanted to help...I thought it would look nice on that...what do you call it? The étagère." She pointed at the metal shelf next to the register.

"I know you thought that, honey, but don't you see that it's full of other white things?"

Bonnie had, actually, seen exactly that. That's why she'd thought the candle would fit in. "Yeah."

"That candle would pull the focus away from the orb, don't you see that? Go sit, sweetie. I'll handle this customer and then make you a cup of coffee. You look exhausted."

The orb. What was an orb? That round fountain thing? Who needed an orb? It wasn't even an antique—most of the stuff in here wasn't. Most of it was crap from China, home decorating stuff her mother picked up in San Francisco on her mega stock sprees. And the tourists loved it. All of it. The more crap her mother piled into the store, the more flew out on the wings of dollar bills. Older men with sad eyes and lots of money bought the chairs some general (might have) sat in, and young women with shining eyes and new, flashy rings bought the knickknacks. Bonnie loved to sit in the plush red armchair at the back of the shop and watch her mother work. Nobody in town could beat Marge at the hard upsell. *Oh, isn't this teacup sweet? It's too bad it's just a single cup. Did you see the Royal Halsey tea set on this shelf here? Isn't it gorgeous? Totally intact. I know you only want the one cup, but I just have to tell you a story about when my mother gave me my first tea party on the back lawn of her house. It started to rain, and instead of whisking me and my stuffed animals indoors, she held three umbrellas over our heads as I continued my party... that set looked so much like this one. Oh, it just makes me miss her even more. All right, let me ring up that poor little orphan teacup for you.*

The entire set would be bought, of course, and the single cup would go back into pride of place, living to lure another sucker the next day.

The funny thing was that Bonnie had asked her mother once, "Where is that old tea set now?"

"What?"

"The tea set Gramma held the umbrellas over?"

Marge had laughed. "Oh, honey, that was just a story. I had chronic bronchitis as a kid, she would never have let me be outside in a rainstorm. Besides, remember how she only used plastic plates? She liked things to be unbreakable."

Now, she listened to her mother suggest to a woman

holding a small baby that the hand-knitted christening gown would be the thing that made her mother-in-law take her seriously. "Is she overbearing? Oh, yes, my mother-in-law was, too. Let me tell you how I won her over to my side…It was with a gown much like this, in fact." Bonnie's mother never even knew her own mother-in-law—she had died years before she married Bonnie's father.

Marge Maddern told a good whopper. And everyone loved her for it, including her daughter. It was comforting to hear them retold—those bedtime, big-fish stories.

They were what she needed to hear. Bonnie had a sinking feeling that wouldn't go away. Her heart felt like it was located somewhere below her bellybutton. The chief had yelled at them for being *children*. They were so stupid. *She* was so stupid, it wasn't just Caz. They'd both known better. Who argued like that, in front of everyone? She was so disappointed in herself, and that was the hardest part.

Bonnie yawned and rubbed her eyes, trying to push back both the embarrassment of her actions and the sadness of the last call of the shift. She'd gotten off duty at eight that morning after a busy night—they'd had four calls after midnight, back to back. Two had been simple difficulty breathing, one had been a fall, but one had been a forty-year-old guy who just woke up dead. Well, his girlfriend had woken up, anyway. Shelley told them she'd kissed his cheek when her alarm went off and found his skin cold. Judging by lividity and body temp, he'd probably died shortly after they'd gone to bed the night before. "All night?" Shelley kept gasping. "He was dead all night? And I was right next to him? I could have saved him. That means I killed him. I *killed* him." Her eyes had been so wide and panicked. "I killed the man I loved."

She'd done nothing of the sort. The man had epilepsy,

and even though he'd been on his meds, he'd probably had a massive seizure and just stopped breathing. "It wasn't your fault," Bonnie had said over and over. "It was good you were with him. That's what matters. You were with him."

"I wasn't," Shelley gasped. "I was *asleep*. When he needed me most. I slept through losing him. We're getting married in a week. How can I—?"

Caz had been primary on that run—there had been no arguing about that for the rest of their tour. They'd taken turns, no discussion. Once they'd decided they wouldn't transport the patient's body to the hospital and the cops got on scene and called the coroner, technically there was no need for the ambulance to stay on scene, but in unspoken agreement, they sat with Shelley, Caz on one side of her, Bonnie on the other. Bonnie handed her tissues and rubbed her back. When the woman fell sideways, sobbing so hard she could barely breathe, Caz caught her, wrapping his arms around her. Their eyes had met over her head, and Caz had such a *look*. It was as if he were feeling Shelley's pain with her, as if he'd feel it for her if he could.

Bonnie had wanted to touch his arm then. It was such a surprising feeling she'd stayed still and dropped her eyes to the woman mourning between them.

Bonnie knew Shelley wouldn't remember a minute of it later. She'd never know they were there, and if they ran into her at the grocery store, she'd smile vaguely at them, unsure why their faces made her feel like crying. That was the way it should be. Bonnie and Caz were there for support, until Shelley's mother arrived. When she did, they left quietly.

They didn't talk in the rig on the way back to the station. After they pulled in and finished cleanup, Caz had simply said, "We need to talk about the fundraiser."

"I know," she said.

"Next shift."

"Yeah." Their eyes hadn't met again. They hadn't said goodbye. They'd just walked away from each other.

Bonnie had gone straight from the station to her mother's house. Marge hadn't looked surprised to find her daughter on the sofa when she wandered through the house.

"Bad night?" was all her mother had said.

"I guess."

Marge said simply, "Your father's sleeping. Want to come with me to the store?"

"Of course I do."

"Coffee. Then we'll go."

Two hours after Darling Trinkets opened, Bonnie was almost ready to head home for a real nap. She waited until her mother finished telling a customer a story about how that exact brand of electric candle had prompted a marriage proposal once, and then said, "Hey, Mom. I'm gonna split."

"Dinner tonight?"

Bonnie wanted to. That was the embarrassing part. She was thirty-one. She had plenty of friends, both in the department and out. Mike, a systems analyst she'd been dating off and on for six months, wanted to go to the movies tonight. Then he would want to make out and maybe more, and all Bonnie could think of when she pictured his face was *yawn*. What she really wanted to do was spend the day with her mother at the store and then lounge on her parents' back patio and watch her father char burgers into lumps of coal while he made the same dumb jokes that he'd been making her entire life. *What's brown and sticky, daughter?* A pause. *A stick!*

She almost never reacted to bad calls this way. In the fire service, you weren't supposed to take things home. And for the most part, Bonnie didn't. She could run three DOAs and then have dinner, more worried about whether they were almost out of steak sauce than how the new widows were doing. Compartmentalizing was part of the job.

But the woman who woke up with her boyfriend not breathing next to her—Shelley—wasn't leaving her for some reason. The panicked look of terror, which Shelley had worn for the first hour they were there, had given way to emptiness by the time they'd driven away. Shelley's mother had arrived and had wrapped her arms around her daughter, but instead of falling to the floor in wails—as Bonnie had seen so many times before—Shelley stayed stock still, swaying rigidly as she appeared to hold her mother up. Her eyes had been blank, her gaze bleak.

What would it be like, to love so hard you became a shell of a person when you lost that love?

"I'm not sure. Mike and I might have plans..." Quickly, just for a second, Bonnie saw Caz's pale blue eyes in her mind.

Her mother smiled. "Ditch that guy and have burgers with us. Cheesy fries on bacon burgers. Your favorite."

"I can't do that..."

"You're not the slightest bit serious about him. A mother knows."

Well, there was really nothing to say to that. Her mother was right. She *wasn't* serious. She was just killing time with Mike.

"Tell me what happened last night." Marge dropped into the soft chair next to Bonnie.

"Why do you think something happened?"

"Because you have that look."

"Which one?" Bonnie tried to put her expression back in order.

"Your sad one."

"I'm not *sad*." Sadness was for other people. Bonnie was cheerful. Chipper. Always positive. That was, literally, her job.

Marge just looked at her, her dark eyebrows raised.

Fine. "Okay, we lost a guy this morning."

"I'm sorry, honey."

Bonnie felt something burn the backs of her eyes. It was surprising and unwelcome. She might feel things sometimes, but she never *cried*. Crying was what normal people did. Not firefighters, not paramedics. "Yeah."

"How old?"

"Forty. We didn't even work him up. He was cold when we got there."

"Married?"

"Girlfriend. Fiancée. They were getting married in a week."

Marge covered her mouth and said softly, "Oh."

"Her face..." Bonnie took a deep, slow breath. "I'm not sure I've ever seen someone lose someone they were so in love with. I mean, I've seen hundreds of people lose their spouses, and it's always terrible. But to be so excited..."

Her mother nodded. "About the life in front of them, and then to lose that."

"I just can't imagine."

"That's the problem with your job. You don't have to imagine it. The rest of us have to watch fake stuff on TV and cry about it. You actually have to see it, day in, day out. What if you....what if you went to see someone?"

Bonnie felt an ache behind her eyes. "What, like a therapist? No."

"It's nothing to be ashamed of. I could help you find someone..."

"We have counseling at work if we need it. I don't need it."

One eyebrow arched—her mother had always been able to convey a whole book with just that one eyebrow. "You've used it how many times?"

Never. Her mom knew that.

"All I'm saying is, think about it. It's there for a reason."

"Meh." Bonnie shook herself. "I'm fine. Thanks for listening. That's all I needed, just a Mom-ear for a minute. I'm going to go home and catch some sleep."

Marge stood. "Come over tonight?"

"Can I say maybe?"

"I'm sure you have the ability to do so," her mother said crisply. The doorbell chimed as three new customers piled into the store giving early exclamations of delight over the Darling Bay tea towels (decorated with the town's iconic pier).

"But I think you should say yes." Her mother kissed her on the cheek, and Bonnie jumped in surprise. Their family wasn't demonstrative—they weren't the kind to hug and kiss. They didn't say *I love you*. So the kiss undid Bonnie a little. Something prickled behind her eyes.

She hurried out of the store, hoping her mother hadn't noticed.

CHAPTER 7

Caz muttered a curse. He wasn't trying to protect his father's ears—God knew Tony Lloyd had been the man who taught Caz what a true swearfest was. But his dad hadn't spoken in almost a year now. It wouldn't be fair to say the words his father had loved to utter in front of him when he couldn't repeat them back with satisfaction.

His father had always been the best curser ever. He could make a bunkhouse full of cowboys blush like school-girls with his creative sentences that normally centered around the kind of hell the men would go to if they didn't get the herd branded in time for market, or if they let one more coyote take down a calf.

Now Tony Lloyd was in a wheelchair during the day and in a hospital bed at night. His eyes stayed open when he was awake, but there was no awareness behind them. His full-time caretaker, Joyce Castro, said that she could tell what he wanted by the tilt of his mouth, but Caz thought she was full of it. His father had been the strongest man he'd ever known. To see him reduced to this—slack jawed and empty eyed—Caz was just glad his dad was too out of it to really understand his own state.

He and Joyce eased Tony into the wheelchair. Caz placed a small wooden horse he'd whittled at work into his father's lap. Sometimes it seemed to help, something for Tony to hold, to work his fingers over.

"There," Joyce said. "You got your horsie now. You're gonna feel great today, Mr. Tony. Just great. It's your son's day to take care of you, and I know those are your favorite days."

Caz knew they were *her* favorite days, her days off. She lived at the ranch in a room next to Tony's, so she'd be back tonight, but two days a week, Joyce went into Darling Bay and saw her daughter and her friends. It was only fair. Everyone needed days off.

It hadn't stopped Caz from wanting to hire another part-time nurse for those two days.

That would be stupid. He was a paramedic. Tony was *his* father, after all.

"I think we should go sit on the porch this morning," Joyce said. "It's supposed to be spring out there, but it feels like summer's coming. Would you like that, Mr. Tony?"

As if he would answer. Caz pushed the chair, moving it smoothly across the old hardwood floors, over the planks his father had put in by hand. In a movie, his father would wake up every once in a while and say something soul-stirring. Sadly, though, this wasn't a movie. Or if it was, it was the worst one he'd ever had to sit through.

Today, Caz would spend the day on the covered porch with his father. He'd read an old paperback Western out loud, not because he thought his father cared, but because he hated it to be so quiet, with nothing but the harsh sounds of his father's breathing to break the day into manageable pieces.

"You go have a good day off, Joyce." He tried to mean it.

"Okay, I will. He had a rough night last night. He might be tired today."

Like father, like son, Caz figured. They'd lost a guy this morning who was supposed to get married on Saturday. He'd sat with the girlfriend on the couch for a while. It had been terrible.

Bonnie had held the woman's hand, she'd said those things that women always said, over and over. "There, there. We're here. It's going to be okay. We're here. It's okay."

That was the problem with women—they didn't tell the truth.

It *wouldn't* be okay for Shelley. It would probably never be okay again. Bonnie telling her it would didn't help anything.

Words never helped. They only hurt. He'd learned that young from his mother when she'd playfully asked, *Who do you love more, Caswell? Me or your father?* He'd said the wrong thing, thinking of the way his father let him sit on the horses saddle-less, the way his father let him hold his best carving knife. It had been a lie—he'd loved her the most, with her soft hands and the way she kissed him goodnight, the way her eyes lit to see him each and every time. Caz had been teasing his mother. Of course he loved her best.

His mother had left after his flippant lie, had left the ranch and her husband and her kid, to go find stardom. Tony Lloyd had raised Caz the best he could on his own, which included TV dinners and a lot of swearing. Words had chased away Caz's mother, and words—all the words he'd been able to fit into his letters to her in Nashville—hadn't brought her back. She'd died there of an overdose, still trying to get a record deal. Sometimes Caz wondered how good the medics had been who'd responded to the call. How hard had they worked to try to save her? Did they know how incredible her voice was? She'd have been the next big star if she'd lived. Probably. If Caz hadn't chased her away.

Caz and his father both hated country music.

Now, Joyce waved as she walked down the driveway and got in the pickup Caz had given her last year when her ancient Ford had broken down for the last time on the long driveway to the ranch. She hadn't wanted to take it from him, but what the heck was he supposed to do with his dad's old work truck? Sell it? It was tired, too, just like his dad, without quite as many miles. The truck was safe, even if it made funny noises, and it ran. He was glad someone was using it.

Caz wondered—briefly—what kind of car Bonnie had. He'd only ever seen her arrive at work on a bicycle, which was kind of ridiculous given that they stayed at the station for forty-eight hours at a time. All of them lugged bags in with them when they came, fresh clothing, bedding (if they hadn't gotten around to washing it at the station), and food, because even though they theoretically ate together, everyone had different food requirements. Caz liked a couple of handfuls of mixed nuts for breakfast instead of eggs, and sometimes he ate the same thing for lunch with a banana. Food was fuel. He couldn't be bothered to think hard about it more than once a day, whereas some of the guys seemed to need to cook something on the stove three and four times a day.

Bonnie, he'd noticed, loved the breads. All of them. No gluten-free silliness from her, which was refreshing. She made pancakes in the morning, feeding them to whoever walked by, then she ate a double-decker sandwich for lunch. If it was her turn to cook, she always made pasta—something extra rich with lots of cheese, and of course, heavily loaded garlic bread on the side. Carbs plus carbs and then more carbs. No wonder she rode her bike to work, now that he thought about it.

She was a good cook, he had to admit. He looked forward to her nights of cooking way more than he did the nights of some of the other guys. Guy Mazanti seemed to think dinner was an iceberg lettuce salad with a rack of barbecue ribs. Well, of course, minus the salad, that wasn't a bad dinner.

Work. Dang it. He wished he hadn't thought about it, hadn't thought about *her*. Lately, it seemed like he was doing too much of that. He'd only been her partner for a month, and she was taking up way too much space in his brain.

And what in the blazes were they going to do about that fundraiser?

Caz thought long and hard before digging his cell phone out of his pocket. He made sure his father was covered warmly enough. He offered him some water, which his father managed better than he usually did. As his father fell asleep on the deck, Caz ran his fingers idly over the wooden rail of the porch. He should sand it down, put another coat of paint on. Maybe in the summer he'd do that. His father was fine, snoring lightly in his chair, so Caz wandered around the big house and back to the deck of the little cottage he'd been staying in. Joyce had said she should stay with them, in the front house, but this cottage had been the first thing Caz had ever built with his own two hands. He and his father had planned it, raised the walls and put on the roof (which could use redoing, he noticed. He'd do that as soon as the spring rains were done). Building the cottage had put the need in his hands to keep building.

He missed his mostly-built cabin up north so much it sometimes hurt.

But this was where he was. At least until his father didn't need taking care of anymore.

Caz sat on the bottom step in front of his cottage, his boots splayed out into the dust below. The sunlight was thin but warm. Then he dialed the number Bonnie had insisted he program into his phone.

Bonnie answered on the second ring. "You! If I said I was surprised, that would be an understatement. What's up?"

"I don't really want to work with you on the fundraiser." As an opening statement, it wasn't the greatest one he'd ever led with, Caz knew. But by then the words were out.

There was a pause. Then Bonnie said, "Look. I was working on my bike. It's my day off. Do I really have to put up with this today?"

"But we do have to work together on this, and we have to do well. This is important to me. It's a good cause." He wouldn't tell her about his father, about how hard every single day off was.

"Yeah, yeah. Sure. I know. Alzheimer's. Great cause. Also, I just want to get the chief off our backs. I want him to forget how mad he is at us. It would be even *better* if he got pissed at someone else. You think we can make that happen? Because I think we can. We just have to come up with some great ideas." Her voice was so light and cheerful he wanted to crawl through the phone and wrap himself in that sound. What would it be like to feel that way all the time? Sometimes when he passed her in the hallway at work, when her blond hair was still sticking straight up from running her hands through it, her smile was so bright it almost blinded him.

"Let's meet," he said. "Tomorrow." Joyce would be back to watch Dad and he could sneak away for a few hours.

"Meet? On our day *off*?"

He didn't answer.

Eventually, she sighed. "Okay, but let's ride bikes."

"I'll be fine in my truck, but you feel free to ride whatever you want." *Save a horse, ride a cowboy.* When he was a teenager, he'd had that old bumper sticker on his first beat-up pickup truck.

"No." There was a laugh in her voice. "I want *you* to ride a bike, too. That's the point. You have one, don't you?"

Somewhere in the barn was his old mountain bike, probably stuck under a tarp, spider webs wrapping the spokes. "I do, but..."

"Ride it. You live out Route 119, don't you?"

No way was she coming to the ranch. "Look..."

"So we meet halfway. Hold on. I'm going inside the house. Let me look it up." There was the slam of a door and then the sound of a keyboard clattering. "Oh, perfect. Bud's Bar out where Lazy Creek joins the main road. Looks like it's about five miles from both of us."

"That's a bar."

"Give the man his prize! You don't have to drink, my friend, but I'm telling you, the beers are cold and the burgers are *amazing*."

She called him a friend.

They weren't friends. At least, not that he knew of.

Bonnie went on. "Unless you don't think you can ride ten miles round trip your first time back out?"

"I can ride ten miles." Caz sure hoped he could.

"Great. Tomorrow, one o'clock. Don't forget your

sunscreen!" She laughed, a bright jingle of happiness, and then her voice was gone.

Caz held out his cell phone. He looked at it as if he'd never seen it before. Flat, matte black on one side, shiny on the other. Great reception. It was a good phone. A champion of a phone.

In fact, he didn't think he'd ever had a better phone in his life. He kind of felt like kissing it, but that would officially be the dumbest thing he'd ever done in his life, so he just put it back in his pocket and went around the house to make sure his father was all right.

CHAPTER 8

Bonnie sat at an outdoor picnic table with a beer and her book. It hadn't been as hilly as she'd thought it was, and she'd made it faster than she'd planned.

That wasn't a problem—she always packed a paperback in one of her panniers, for exactly this kind of situation. The sun was breaking through a thin layer of fog and it was warm enough on her shoulders. The beer was bold and hoppy. If only she didn't have dealing with Caz on her list of things to do today, it would be just about perfect.

Speak of the devil.

Caz came into view at the bottom of the dirt driveway that wound through the live oaks and led to the porch at Bud's Bar. The hill he had to climb was no joke. Bonnie hadn't had to get off and walk, but she'd come close to it, and she rode her bike every day. He was going to struggle with it.

And she had a ringside seat. Bonnie grinned and settled back, the wood warming her skin through her thin T-shirt.

But good grief.

The man didn't struggle.

Wearing a blue T-shirt and board shorts, Caz had to stand up on the pedals to make them turn, but he took the hill faster than she had. And the man's calves...The closer he got, the more impressive they looked. They were solid roped muscle. She could probably cut an apple on the back of his leg. Even his thighs, where she could see them under the shorts, looked strong as the wood he whittled on the patio at work.

When Caz stopped short at her table, fishtailing his bike with a small flourish, she laughed.

"Not too shabby."

Caz took his helmet off his head with one thumb. "Oh, come on. Admit it. You're impressed with an old guy like me."

"How old are you?" She had, in fact, assumed he was older than she was, but only because at the station he acted that way. And there had never been much call for her to examine his calves—those amazing calves, the way his gastrocnemius met his soleus—when they were at work.

"Thirty-four."

Only three years older than she was. "Oh, yeah, *such* an old man. That explains the board shorts."

Caz looked down in surprise. "These are Quiksilver. They're the bomb."

"You saying that proves my point."

"The kids don't say bomb anymore?"

"I don't think they ever said it much in the first place."

"Shoot." Then he reached for her beer, and without asking, lifted it to his mouth and swallowed. She would have objected, would have yelled at him for not asking first, just the same way she would have at any of the other guys from the station—that was, she *would* have if she hadn't been so busy ogling the underside of his jaw. He hadn't shaved today, and she'd never seen his stubble so thick, even when they had to go out on five a.m. medical runs. He hadn't shaved this morning at all, it looked like. And the way he swallowed hard, making his Adam's apple bob—she couldn't take her eyes off him.

This was *Caz*.

Her work nemesis. She'd never thought of him as sexy (okay, never that she would admit to herself). Caz was too quiet, too reserved. Too *grumpy*. She liked men who were loud and irreverent and happy. Her last boyfriend had been an auctioneer and he'd had the pipes to prove it. Mike, while he couldn't be called a boyfriend—he'd barely seemed to care when she'd canceled on him earlier in the week— talked more than any other guy she'd ever met, about nothing at all. Caz barely spoke.

But right now? His not speaking was okay. She kind of just...wanted to watch.

He plunked the bottle back onto the tabletop. "Thanks. Just what I needed. I've got the next round."

"I'll say you do. Not even asking first. Sheesh." But there was no sting in her tone. Bonnie honestly didn't mind. And when she swigged from the neck, she thought she could taste the salt from his lips on the cool glass.

Silly.

She waved her hand. "I already ordered my burger. You should do the same. Tell Bud we're together." The words sounded funny coming out of her mouth. "I mean, that we're going to eat together...so he can get the food out at the same time..." She was making it worse. "And I'll take another one of these since you drank half of mine."

Was that a smile on his normally stiff face? She didn't want to analyze it, and stuck her nose back into her book as he strode off.

When he returned outside minutes later, he held out a new bottle.

"Thanks."

"You bet," he said. They clinked bottle necks, and sat back, looking down at the road below. He sat next to her, so they could both watch the view. A swirl of colored leaves that had somehow made it through the winter rains stirred, and a single truck rose a plume of dust as it raced down 119. An unseen bird screeched a raucous love song over their heads.

"You look..." Bonnie paused, tilting her head.

He glanced up at the blue sky. "Sunburned? I forgot the sunscreen you warned me about."

"I have some in my bag, I'll give you some before we leave. No, you look..." What was it? Why did he look so different? Was it just because he wasn't wearing his uniform? That couldn't make such a difference, could it? She was used to sitting next to Caz. She sat next to him in the rig for hours and hours at a time. What *was* it?

"Eh. Ranching'll get you burned just as fast. I'm usually a little browner, but I haven't been in the fields as much as usual since I took the job at Darling Bay."

Relaxed. That's what it was. He looked easy in his skin, not all tight at the eyes like he did at work. "You loved riding here."

He shook his head. "Nah."

"You did."

"It was okay."

"You *loved* it." Bonnie knew that look—she had the same look herself sometimes. "You love being on a bike, too."

The right side of his face cracked into a smile. "I guess it didn't suck."

"I knew it! When was the last time you rode?"

"A long time."

"How long?"

He sighed and tilted his head back, closing his eyes against the sun. Bonnie had to fight the urge to reach out to see if that stubble was exactly as rough as it looked. "Maybe high school."

"You're kidding!" She gazed at the mountain bike. "But that looks so good."

"Cleaned it. I had to replace both tubes and nothing on it had been oiled since I was seventeen. Bits of old rubber were flying off as I rode, and I bet something goes wrong with the shifter on the way home—it was being a pain on the ride here."

"It's your high school bike!"

His smile grew. He was doing a dismal job of hiding it behind the beer bottle.

"What was her name? Your bike?"

"It didn't have a *name*."

"You were a teenager. It totally had a name."

"Don't remember."

"I know you do."

"If I tell you, will you leave me alone about it?"

"Maybe."

"Betsy."

Bonnie choked on her swig of beer. Foam rose behind her teeth. "Oh, my gosh."

"What? I know it's stupid, but I was a kid."

"That's *my* bike's name."

Caz shook his head. "No, you promised to leave me alone about it. You're not supposed to razz me about my teenage mistakes."

"No, really. My bikes have *always* been named Betsy. Since I was a kid."

"Why?"

"I have no idea." She didn't. The name had just come to her for her first banana-seat bike, and she'd moved the name along with the rear lights whenever she'd upgraded. "What do you call your truck?"

"I don't."

A spear of enjoyment shot through Bonnie's rib cage. This was *fun*. She hadn't expected this. "Are you lying to me?"

"I don't lie."

"You really don't have a name for your truck?"

"Sorry to let you down. What do you call your car?"

"I don't have one."

He met her eyes, and Bonnie felt a jolt that had nothing to do with the way the wind shifted at that moment. "Seriously?"

"Have you ever seen me roll up in one?"

Caz shook his head.

"Why would I need one?"

"I don't know. People just...need cars. Everyone knows that."

"I drive all the time at work," Bonnie said. "You know that. On my days off, I don't need to. I can do everything on my bike." She couldn't help adding proudly, "I even once moved apartments on my bike. Box by box."

"What about your couch? Your bed?"

Bonnie scratched the sweating beer label lightly. "Movers. I make a decent wage. I can afford to hire them when I need them."

"That's just weird. I never knew a Californian without a car."

She shrugged. The conversation was so surprisingly enjoyable that she felt she should change the subject, get back on solid footing with him. "Now you do. What are we doing about this fundraiser?"

Bud, a tiny man with a high bush of white hair, brought out their burgers, grumbling about the walk outside he had to make to bring them. "Shouldn't a put out these tables, more work than they're worth..."

Bonnie watched him retreat and then laughed. "I felt like apologizing, but he did go and put these out here for customers—he just hates when we use them."

Caz bit into the burger, and again, Bonnie was surprised with how enjoyable it was to *watch* him. Maybe she'd been averting her eyes at work when she should have been taking in the show. The muscles in the side of his jaw worked steadily, rhythmically. Something in her heart jumped.

"What?" he said.

"What what?" Bonnie reached for a fry. Okay, five fries. She jammed them into her mouth like it was a contest.

"Why are you staring at me?"

"You're a messy eater." She didn't live with eight men two days a week for nothing. "You're kind of a slob, in fact."

He looked surprised, his dark eyebrows jumping toward his hairline. "I am?"

Bonnie reached forward and used her thumb to wipe an imaginary stain from his chin. "Yep. Big slob. Mustard." She didn't expect the jolt of electricity she felt as she touched his skin. It almost hurt.

Caz reached up and grasped her hand. He peered at the thumb that had just touched his cheek.

Bonnie wanted to draw back, and at the same time, she wanted to see exactly what he was going to do next.

"I don't see mustard here."

"Well…"

His gaze met hers. Something made the air thick between them. "Some might say you just wanted to touch me."

"I—" Bonnie couldn't find the words she needed. It was usually so easy for her to mouth off to anyone. She barely had to try. But with this guy, right now… she had nothing.

"Not that *I* would say that," he went on. "You obviously don't want to touch me. And I don't want to do this." He released her hand and raised his own. He touched her neck and then slid his fingers behind her neck. "And you sure as hell don't want me to do this."

Then Caz, her work partner, the man she wasn't even sure if she liked as a person, kissed her full on the mouth.

CHAPTER 9

He was losing his mind. That was the only explanation for what drove Caz to kiss *Bonnie*, of all people. She was his coworker. Even worse, she was nothing like him. She couldn't understand him if he drew her a map.

But the skin at the back of her neck was as smooth as sanded mahogany, and her mouth was perfect under his. She gave a sharp, electric gasp that sent a jolt all the way through him, right down to his toes. But she didn't draw away. She kissed him back, raising her hand to grasp his wrist. If she'd wanted to, she could have pushed him away with that hand. Instead, she drew him closer to her, meeting his mouth with so much heat Caz wondered if it were possible for him to burst into flame out here in the spring sun.

Her taste was sweet—dill and hops and something else that he wanted more of—so much *more*. What started out sweet moved to erotic almost instantly. What was hot went solar. Her tongue met his, matching him, and raising him. The harder he kissed her, the harder she wound her fingers in her hair. He wasn't even sure how it had happened—had he dragged her to him? Had she jumped?—but she was in his lap, one leg hooked over his, and he knew that she'd be able to feel exactly how steamed up he was getting.

A motorcycle roared up the dirt driveway, and was then followed by another, then three more. They kept coming until the small parking lot was full of guys wearing black leather.

Bonnie pulled back with another one of those sharp gasps, the sound that cut right through him, as if she were dragging a finger down his spine. She wriggled off his lap and back to her seat next to him. In the sunlight, Caz shivered.

Two of the men whooped as a woman rode up the driveway. Bonnie touched her bottom lip—wet from his own mouth—and stared at the riders. "Saved by the...gang, I suppose."

Caz cast a quick look at the interlopers, hating them for riding up right when it was getting good. "I think those are lawyers."

"No."

"Look at the way that one guy's hair is cut." He pointed, but carefully, so the man wouldn't notice. They probably were a gang of lawyers, but hey, there was no reason to tick off any kind of gang, especially the litigious kind.

"That is a nice haircut."

He smiled at her, refusing to think about the way his insides felt—as if there were something flapping around inside his gut that wasn't just the burger and beer. "Dare you to tell him that."

Bonnie laughed but didn't meet his eyes. "Oh, no. Never dare me to do anything."

"Why not?"

"Because I'll do it."

"Good to know."

"No, no. Uh-uh. That's not for you to use. I told you that as a friend. Not for you to use at work."

There she went again with the whole friend thing. "So I can't dare you to drive the rig and let me be primary on every single call?"

She shook her head which gleamed bright in the sun. "Doesn't work that way."

"Why not?"

"Because." She crossed her arms in front of her and scowled, and she looked so dang cute he couldn't help laughing at her.

"Because?"

"Because I make the rules."

"Ah," Caz said. "Only child, right?"

She narrowed her eyes and stared at him. Beside her, a small brown sparrow hopped onto the table and pecked at her leftover hamburger bun. "You don't ask me a thing while we're in the ambulance, you ignore almost everything I say, you never speak a word at the station except pass the salt, and now you're playing twenty questions with me? What gives, Lloyd?"

He wanted to laugh again. The feeling in his chest—that lightness—was something he hadn't felt in a really long time. Just like sitting in this thin spring sunlight felt good, so did the urge to grin at her. It felt good right down to his bones. "Just because you never shut up and I never talk doesn't mean I'm not listening, Maddern. Anybody ever call you Mad?"

"Not anyone who wants to keep all their teeth."

"Good, Mad it is. Sisters? Brothers?"

She narrowed her eyes at him. "You tell *me*, smarty-pants. Do I or do I not have any siblings?"

"I was going to say you didn't, but now that I think about it, you argue too well to be an only. You have one. A sister. Younger."

"Wrong! She's older!"

"Ah, you're the baby. Is she in town?"

"She used to be, but she moved to Los Angeles recently. I miss her."

Her eyes were sad, echoing her statement. What would that be like, to miss a sibling? Caz said, "And you bother your mother at that store you pointed out to me."

"What?"

"Isn't that what she tells you you're doing?"

"Well, yeah, but I'm *helping*. It's not my fault I'm not good at organizing tchotchkes."

"And you hang out with your dad while he grills burgers and makes bad jokes."

Bonnie looked nominally impressed. "Okay, smart guy. What have I been doing with my backyard?"

"Sunbathing naked?"

"No!"

Well, it had been worth a shot. "You're building a tree house out of lumber you and your dad found at the dump." When she'd mentioned it, he'd had to clench his teeth together to stop from asking her what she was using to build it. Reclaimed wood or new plywood? Were the nails galvanized? Were the countersunk screws blued or passivated?

Bonnie sat back, and slapped her hands on her thighs. "Holy cats. You *are* listening to me. Why don't you talk back to me, then?"

He shrugged. "I'm not sure you've ever asked me anything directly."

"That's not possible." She covered her mouth briefly with her hand. "I'm not that rude. Is that true?"

Caz shook his head. "Nah, you've asked me plenty of things."

"So..."

"I'm just...private."

She lifted her shoulders and then dropped them again. "I can respect that." Color lit the tops of her cheeks. Caz could practically hear her remembering the kiss they'd just shared. She went redder and he liked it, liked that he could shake her up.

Because he felt shaken, too. He didn't want to be alone in this.

"Anyway," she said, touching her top lip gently and glancing over at the group on motorcycles. "We should do what we came here to do."

Which was not kissing.

"Yeah." From his pocket, Caz took out a small notebook and a pencil stub.

"How cute," she said. Was that a smirk on her face as she got out her iPhone?

"Don't have to charge this, do I?" he said.

"Oh, yeah? Where's your pencil sharpener?"

She had a point. He would ignore that. "Okay. How are we going to make more money than has ever been raised for the Darling Bay Alzheimer's Support Initiative before?"

"Two words for you, buddy. No, three."

"Yeah?"

Bonnie's lips curved so sweetly he wanted to kiss her again. He couldn't. He wouldn't.

She said, "Truth or Dare."

Without thinking, he said, "Dare." Maybe she'd dare him to kiss her again. He'd do it. He'd do anything she told him to at this moment.

But instead she laughed. "No, Truth or Dare as a

fundraiser. I was always scared of that game, but that's what made it fun. I always picked truth, because...oh, I shouldn't admit this."

He was intrigued. "What?"

"Because I was a good liar as a kid. I could say that I'd been...kissed..." Bonnie's cheeks went red again. "And no one could prove that I...hadn't. Whereas if I'd been dared to kiss someone, I would have had to do it, and..." She pushed her hair off her forehead and blew out a short breath. "Why are we talking about this again? Oh, yeah. If we got firefighters on the stage to play with people pledging amounts to get them to do silly things, the crowd would love it. It would work, right?"

"Silly things like kissing?"

"*No*. This is work." But her voice was breathy. "Seriously. Let's plan this, okay?"

Plan it and get out of here. Back to real life. Back to the ranch, and his drooling father, and the fact that he was a hundred miles from the cabin he wished he'd never had to leave. She was right. Caz would treat this like work. It *was* work. He'd forget that it was nothing but fun to be sitting with Bonnie Maddern outside, watching her drop bits of her hamburger bun on the ground for the group of sparrows that were now cheeping at her feet.

He'd forget that for a few long moments he'd wanted to be here, with her, more than anywhere else on earth.

CHAPTER 10

The dorm at Station One was long and narrow. While some of the newer stations in Darling Bay had individual rooms for the firefighters to sleep in, Station One was old-school with its bed cubicles cordoned off by heavy drapes. Really, the dorm was nothing more than a wide hallway, with narrow single beds on either side of the aisle, but when Bonnie was in the station, she imagined that her little bunk space was her own. Even though in two days B shift would have it and Bruno Sipes would be sleeping in the bed she occupied today, and two days after that, Mariana Bell would be covering the same mattress with her Snoopy sheets, right now, the bed was hers. Tonight, when they all went to sleep, hoping for a peaceful night, Bonnie would pretend she couldn't hear Guy snoring and that Luke didn't fart in his sleep as much as he did.

There was no privacy in a fire station that ran an engine, a truck, and a medic, as well as housing the battalion chief.

None at all.

That's why Bonnie sat on the edge of her bed after she'd

fluffed her two work pillows to within an inch of their life. After making sure the curtain was safely drawn, she leaned against the thin partition wood and touched her bottom lip. For one long, glorious moment, she let herself remember kissing Caz.

Caz Lloyd, of all people.

First of all, she didn't get involved with coworkers. That was her rule, and it always had been. She'd never dated a fellow coworker, not once. Second of all, he was hot as sin. Wait, that wasn't supposed to be number two. *Correction.* Number two, he was a jerk in the station. Except that he apparently listened and remembered every single thing she'd ever babbled to him about. That wasn't fair. That meant he knew so much (he'd remembered about the tree house!) and she knew nothing about him. Number three, she didn't get involved with coworkers. That was numbers four, five, and six, too.

She flopped backward and looked up at the spider web that draped the dim overhead light again, even though she'd taken it down last tour.

Think, Maddern. If she was so sure how she felt on this topic, why did she keep thinking about him? About the way he'd tasted? About the wave of heat that shot through her entire body as his lips took hers strongly, as if they had a right to be there.

Bonnie heard a long sigh, and then realized it was hers.

This had to stop. She needed to come to her senses. Fast.

Dispatch would help.

Lexie was in the middle of reading a recipe. "Hang on," she said. "I think I forgot to add the egg whites."

"Is that what the smell in the kitchen is? Were you

making muffins?" asked Bonnie. "Because those looked like hockey pucks and smelled like socks."

"No, I must have added the egg whites, right? How would I forget something like that?" She closed her eyes and tilted her head backward. Her headset, perennially attached to her ear, swung with her curly red hair. "Slimy. Egg whites. Separating them. I'd remember that, right?"

"Probably."

She snapped her head upright again and fixed her gaze on Bonnie. "Nope, I for sure added them. I remember now."

"What were you trying to make?"

"Coin's daughter Serena's class said that everyone has to take turns being class mom."

"That's kind of sexist, isn't it?"

"It's Coin's turn to be class mom, so no, it isn't, but they asked him to bring in healthy gluten- and sugar-free muffins. Oh, and they have to be vegan. I'm going to have to try it all over again..."

"Then no egg whites." Bonnie glanced over her shoulder at the recipe. "No honey, either."

Lexie looked at her in horror. "What do you *mean*, no honey?"

"Not vegan. You don't want to exploit the bees, do you?"

Bonnie could almost see the expletive about to burst forth from Lexie's lips, but 911 rang. All Bonnie got was a dirty look. Lexie dispatched the medical to Station Three, and gave instructions while the crews were diving. "No tourniquet. Ma'am. Ma'am? Did you hear me? Yes, I'm sure. No tourniquet for your son. He stubbed his toenail. Yes, I know there's a lot of blood, but he's not going to die of it. Yes, I promise. That'll just make it worse." Lexie tapped the side of her headset. "Hello?" She grinned at Bonnie. "I guess she's calling the lawyer for when her child dies of blood loss. Good grief, the kid could have chopped off all his toes and he wouldn't bleed out. But I'm preaching to the choir, right? What's up, lady? What brings you down the hall with a look like that on your face?"

Bonnie touched her cheeks. "What do you mean?"

"You look like you saw a ghost and at the same time, you look all hot and bothered." A voice chattered on the radio and Lexie focused on the screen, hitting her cordless button. "Engine Three, on scene." She released. "Thank goodness. Someone tell that woman to chill the heck out. What's she going to do when he's a teenager? People have to space out their reaction to trauma, otherwise they get all weird too early on. Parents. Sheesh. Oh! The fundraiser. Is that what you're worried about?"

Bonnie nodded, grateful Lexie wasn't focusing on her blush. "Yeah. Well, okay, no. We've kind of got that figured out."

"Already?"

"Yeah. We...met up yesterday and talked."

"Oh!" Lexie looked intrigued. "The silent man of mystery, meeting you outside? Where real people live? What was that like?"

"What do you mean?" Bonnie kept her gaze high, just over Lexie's shoulder, where the laminated map of the district hung.

"Whoa. You *like* him!"

Bonnie felt a burst of adrenaline shoot through to her fingertips, and she felt a deeper blush start at her hairline. "No way."

"You do! You've been riding with him for what, two months? Max? And now you're crushing!"

"I can't stand him." Bonnie thought of the bursts of

static that crackled between them. Earlier in the day, when setting up a backboard for a patient, their hands had touched and Bonnie thought she could almost see the electricity jump from him to her. Her stomach had been in knots all day, but neither of them had mentioned the kiss.

"Mmmm-*hmm*." Lexie leaned forward, lacing her fingers and putting her chin into them. "That's how the best kind starts. I want to be your maid of honor. That is, unless Coin and I elope, which we might, depending on how Serena is acting the week we finally decide to do it. If I'm married, I'll be your matron of honor. Whatever I am, I want to be it."

Bonnie laughed. "Nothing like that is on the horizon. He can barely stand me. It's pretty mutual." *So was that kiss...*

"Don't tell Coin, but I'll admit he's a looker. Ride 'em, cowboy, and all of that."

Bonnie sank into one of the spare dispatch chairs. "So you think he's cute?"

Lexie smiled. "I do. But I don't think he's as cute as *you* think he is, apparently."

"What?"

She waved a hand. "Look at you. Please. It's all over you. You are blissed out on a crush."

"Am *not*." What would Lexie think if she knew that Bonnie had kissed him? To be fair, he'd kissed her first. But she'd definitely been a willing and very active participant. "Okay, maybe a little bit." Bonnie reached forward to clutch desperately at Lexie's arm. "Do you know what a pain in the butt this is going to be? I have to squash it." Saying it out loud was the first time she realized she was so upset about it. "Sitting in the same rig with him for a whole year-long stint?"

"He's junior. He could get moved wherever the chief wants him to go. Maybe he'll move stations on you." Lexie looked dreamy for a moment. "I hope he doesn't, though. He's got that perfect cowboy a—"

"Don't make me think about that. Tell me what to do about it, instead. Tell me how to stop a crush."

Lexie pressed her lips together. Then, as if reminded she had lips, she applied ChapStick while she stared at Bonnie.

Patiently, Bonnie waited.

Instead of answering the question, Lexie said, "What's your fundraiser plan?"

"No, Lex, I need a man plan. I need a get-this-man-out-of-my-system plan. Who cares about the fundraiser? We've got that all worked out."

"This is relevant. Go with me here. What's your fundraising plan? Something delicious? Humiliating? Funny?"

Bonnie sighed and sat back, wincing as the hard plastic of the chair dug into her back. "Maybe all of those. Remember when we were kids, we played Truth or Dare?"

"Of course. I hated that game."

"It was fun," protested Bonnie. Okay, it was fun if you lied and avoided being dared to do anything. "What if we coordinated a pay-for-play Truth or Dare?"

The door to dispatch opened, and Bonnie felt her knees heat up. Caz. Of course.

"Hey, you," said Lexie. "Come in, we were just talking about you."

Oh, jeez...

Caz's voice was low and he didn't meet Bonnie's eyes. "I'm looking for the chief. Do you know where he is?"

Lexie said, "Am I in trouble for something?"

Caz looked surprised. "Um, no..."

"Good." Lexie hit a few keys. "His MDC says he's at the coffee shop. Lousy chief that he is. Didn't even offer to get me a cup."

"Okay..."

"Now, get in here. What do you think of Truth or Dare? Can you explain to me why Bonnie here thinks it's a good idea? The only thing I can think that would be fun about it is if we got firefighters and medics up there and dared them to kiss pigs. Oooh, or each other." Lexie's eyes widened as she looked between the two of them. Bonnie predicted she'd have to kill her soon, probably before the afternoon was over.

Caz said, "We talked about the game, but—"

Bonnie interrupted, "Hey, didn't we have to wash the blankets on the rig? I mean, no one used that last one, but it did hit the floor, and we can't have—"

"I already did it. They're sanitizing now."

"You see?" said Lexie triumphantly. "He's on it. Now. Caz. Old buddy. Old pal. What would you do if someone dared you—for money—to kiss Bonnie over there right on the smacker?"

CHAPTER 11

I t was the last question he'd thought he'd be asked in dispatch. Bonnie had *told* Lexie?

"Really?" He shoved his hands in his uniform pockets and threw a glare in Bonnie's direction. "I can't believe you—"

"I'm just teasing," said Lexie. "*Sheesh.* Okay, so let me talk this out, so I'm sure I understand what the plan is. All right. So we get two firefighters up there on the stage after the dinner portion of the evening."

"Neither of whom will be me." Caz had to look away from Bonnie and the way she bit her lower lip when she was nervous. He couldn't be totally sure he wouldn't reach over and touch that same lip with his forefinger. Right in front of Lexie. Good grief, Bonnie Maddern acted on him like a nerve agent. She should come with a warning placard. A red light should have been flashing outside Dispatch's door, to show people it wasn't safe to enter.

"Shhh. You don't have to go first, if that's what you mean. But yeah, two firefighters up on stage. Okay, they choose whether they want a Truth or a Dare. Then we hold a mini-auction. Whoever collects the most money each round is off the hook, and the other person has to either tell the truth or do the dare in front of everyone."

"Exactly," said Bonnie. "So that means that if the dare is take your shoes off and get a pedicure, Guy Mazanti will work extra hard to raise money in the crowd so his opponent will have to do it instead of him." Everyone knew Guy Mazanti couldn't stand having his feet touched, or even, really, looked at.

"Oh, man, I love the pedicure idea. And I'd like Coin to lose that one, please. I want to see his toes a pretty, pretty pastel pink. With flowers. And maybe rhinestones and glitter!" Lexie looked delighted.

Caz could admit that it would probably raise money. It was a cute idea. If he were a citizen going to a benefit put on by firefighters, he'd probably be into seeing them laughingly humiliated, too.

It's just he didn't want to be one of them up there on the stage. "Sounds good. Sounds funny. And since we're organizing it, we won't have to be on stage."

Bonnie looked at him gratefully, her eyes wide with relief. A man would ride a horse a long way to get a gorgeous blonde to look at him that way, Caz realized. He might even ride a bike to see her, a bike that hadn't been ridden since he was a seventeen-year-old with nothing better to do than mess around on bikes all day.

"Nice try," said Lexie. "This is my show, and you two will be the grand prize."

Caz scrambled to think of something that would dissuade her. "What about the chief? Barger would be great up there. What if we dare him to shave off that mustache?"

Lexie gave him a look of horror. "We don't want to see

what he's got under there. No. He'll have to do something else for a dare. He *is* going to be our opener, though."

Bonnie said, "You think you can make him do that?"

"Please. This is dispatch. We tell *all* y'all what to do. Speaking of which, I need Truth or Dare posters. A bunch of them. Make them big." The 911 line rang, loud and jarring. Lexie answered, looked at the address, and waggled her fingers at them, shooing them out.

"Must be ours," said Bonnie, pushing her way into the hall.

Caz followed her jog to the app bay, unable to keep his eyes off the way her sweet little rear swayed. In the rig, he got in the driver's seat without discussion. He hit the lights and pulled out, headed to the accident Lexie had just dispatched them on. "So, let me get this straight, Mad," he said. "We're being put on poster duty?"

In his peripheral vision, he could see Bonnie smile. "I believe we just got put on that, yes."

"I haven't made a poster since..." He took a sharp turn onto 8th. "Since high school."

"What was the poster for?"

"What?" He whooped the siren. "I don't remember."

"Yes, you do." She had not an ounce of doubt in her voice.

Caz cleared his throat. "Cheer club."

"Cheer club? You mean for the cheerleaders?"

"It was a *club*. My girlfriend made me."

"She made you!"

"I'm telling you, she was mean."

Bonnie laughed.

"Mean like a snake," Caz went on, easing carefully around the Darling Bay Trolley (often full of day trippers who didn't take the time to look before stepping into traffic on their way to the beach). Then he hit the gas again. "Mean like a mama bear who's lost her cub. She said use the puff-paint, I used the puff-paint."

Bonnie's laugh was like alcohol in his blood. He probably shouldn't even be driving. He was over the limit.

"I like you so much better like this," she said, still laughing. "I like you talking. You can be *fun*."

It sobered him quickly. Kiss or no kiss, he was here to get the job done. He couldn't forget that. He wasn't there to have fun. His mother had been one for having fun, all the time, until she'd left. Fun was a way of lying to yourself, and Caz didn't lie.

"Numbers?" he asked.

Bonnie peered at the computer screen, always hard to read in daylight. "861. Should be that red house, right there."

Caz braked too hard. He wasn't here to be *fun*. Not for her or for anyone else. The sooner he remembered that and got over this little infatuation or whatever it was, the better off he'd be.

"Caz, I didn't mean..."

He opened the door and got out, shutting it behind him, closing it on whatever she had to say.

CHAPTER 12

They ran four more calls before sunset. And no matter what she said, Bonnie couldn't get Caz to open up again.

They'd had a moment.

No, not *that* moment—not the kiss at Bud's Bar—even though that was something she couldn't stop thinking about. And while the kiss was a highly interesting thing to think about, she knew it wasn't the most important. *That* had been in the rig, when Caz had made her laugh. It was a small thing, but it was something she and Caz hadn't had yet together. That camaraderie. It's what made the department special. Bonnie's ex-partners were her best friends. Riding the rig together was how you got to really know someone. You saw them save a life, and then you saw them lose someone—you saw them hold an old woman's hand as they told her her husband wasn't going to make it, and you saw them swallow back tears. And then, in the rig, you laughed about the roller-skating tourist who had just eaten it when he tried to skate past the boardwalk onto the sand. That's what partners were for.

It was what she hadn't found in Caz. Not until earlier today. Then he'd gone all prickly again, and while she guessed he would say it was her fault, she wouldn't buy that. She hadn't done anything except tell him she liked him more when he was laughing.

He'd been surly ever since. Such a *man* move.

The night went much the same way—they missed dinner for a call where a woman burned her left pinky while making hard-boiled eggs and even though she had a Mercedes in the driveway and a husband on the couch watching the game, she'd wanted a ride to the hospital, and she'd complained the whole way that they wouldn't put their siren on. When they got back to the station, Tox's dog Methyl had grabbed the ribs the engine guys had left out for them, and she'd eaten every single one, bones and all. Tox was surly with Hank and Coin, and Lexie hadn't slept on her nap and was grumpy on the radio.

Everyone seemed to be in a bad mood, not just Bonnie. Bed was the best place for her. She hoped she got to stay there.

But in bed, Bonnie had never been so aware of how close Caz's body was to hers, separated as they were by only a thin partition cubicle wall, open at the top. Unlike some of her other coworkers, he was normally quiet once he was in bed. Guy Mazanti snored like a semi-truck climbing a steep hill, all wheezes and groans. Hank was a fish-flopper, flipping to one side, then flopping to the next seconds later. Tox didn't snore but breathed so deeply he seemed to suck up all the air in the dorm and then expel it in a huge sigh.

Caz, though, was always quiet. It made her nervous. There was usually a clank of his belt buckle as he took off his uniform pants and changed into his shorts, and then a squeak as he sat on the edge the bed. That was it. Nothing more. He didn't even snore.

Tonight Bonnie hadn't even realized she was waiting for him until she glanced at her watch for the tenth time. It was after midnight, and she still hadn't heard the tell-tale squeak of his bed.

He was probably somewhere in the station, *doing* something. It seemed like he always had something in his hands —if it wasn't work related, it was his whittling. Some of the older guys were threatened by his energy, she knew. The old-timers, the ones retiring within the next couple of years, the ones who had no motivation to promote to a higher rank —they were the ones threatened by men like Caz. Caz showed them that there *was* always something to be done around the firehouse. Even if they hadn't run a call in twenty-hours, the ambulance could always stand some tidying if not a full wash down. There was always laundry. There was always, *always* stainless steel to polish. Old-school guys grumbled from their recliners about new bucks trying to impress the brass.

Bonnie knew, though, that Caz wasn't trying to impress anyone. That should have been obvious to anyone who met him. He might be newish to their department, but not to the fire service itself. He was a man who liked to be busy.

But he usually went to bed at a normal time. It was weird. She kind of...missed him, missed knowing that inches away from her skin, on the other side of the particle board, he slept.

She didn't miss him enough to get up and look for him, though. No way. That would just be...

Bonnie rolled over and whacked her knee on the wall. It was a good thing he *wasn't* in bed or she would have just startled him right out of it. Shutting her eyes tight, she told herself to sleep. Five minutes later, she was still telling herself the same thing. Twenty minutes later, she gave up. What if he was actually hurt somewhere in the station?

Her eyes flew open and she stared into the darkness.

Ridiculous. Thirty-four-year-olds didn't usually die randomly of heart attacks or sudden strokes.

But heck. It did happen. Every once in a very great while, a young guy would trip and fall down, dead. That forty-year-old man the other day, for example. Healthy except for his epilepsy, dead a week before his wedding.

It happened.

Caz could be out in the apparatus bay right now, struggling to breathe, in anaphylactic shock from some brand new allergy, literally dying for someone to save him.

It was probably her moral duty to check.

Putting on her slippers, she sneaked through her curtain without moving it, avoiding the screech of the curtain rings.

The kitchen was dark and still smelled of the ribs Methyl had stolen. No Caz. The dayroom was deserted. She snapped off the television which was playing infomercials on mute to the empty room. She didn't actually go *into* the men's bathroom—some things should stay private—but she could tell by the crack at the door that the lights were out inside. The weight room was dark. The cardio room was empty. The app bay was her next stop, but after checking each rig she knew he wasn't there, either.

Where *was* he? Firefighters and paramedics didn't get to go home on a bad day. You couldn't just leave if you came down with the flu—you had to get coverage before you could leave or you left your whole crew a body short. An engine couldn't go to a fire with two people on board; an ambulance didn't roll with just one person.

You didn't just get to leave the firehouse.

So he was somewhere.

The only two places she hadn't checked were the dispatcher's dorm (no firefighter would *dare*, even Coin, who shared Lexie's bed when they weren't at work) and the outdoor patio where they kept the grill.

And he was there, on the patio. Sitting on an old wooden chair, with his legs kicked up onto the stump of the palm tree they'd cut down the year before when it got struck by lightning, Caz was asleep. At his feet were curled shavings of wood, resting on top of the newspaper he always laid down when he whittled. In his lap was a half-formed wolf—the head and front paws were startlingly clear, the back haunches still uncarved. Caz's cheek was propped on one arm. He looked like someone in a hospital waiting room. She'd seen that look a million times before. Someone too worried to go home and lie down, but too bone-tired to stay awake.

What was Caz Lloyd so worried about?

And geez, wasn't he cold? Bonnie wrapped her arms around herself. It had been a gorgeous, barbecue kind of day, yes, but with night, the air had gone cold again. Without the usual layer of fog for insulation, it was downright chilly outside.

She should leave him.

He was out here for a reason, because he didn't want to sleep inside. *Maybe he didn't want to sleep next to her.*

She turned to go back in.

"Sorry I'm not cracking jokes, Mad."

Bonnie jumped. "I didn't want to wake you."

He shrugged. The dark circles under his eyes were deepened by the yellow light streaming over Bonnie's shoulder. "But then you did."

Her temper frayed at its tired edges. "What's your problem?"

Caz shoved his hand through his hair and it stood up even more angrily than it had been. "Why does everyone in this department ask me that?"

Bonnie stepped forward—ignoring the crackle of electricity that jumped between them—and lowered her voice. There were no windows facing the patio, but the back door to the chief's dorm was just around the corner, and she didn't want Barger to hear them arguing. Again. "Because you're a pain in the ass."

"Excuse me?"

The words had been pent up too long. "You act like you're so much better than the rest of us. You just can't come down to our level, can you?"

"Wait—"

"No, *you* wait. I'm sorry that maybe the move to this department isn't everything you wanted it to be."

"It's—"

"But you're here. Like my mother would say, 'You made this bed, now you have to eat crackers in it.' "

"What?"

"And you've got the ranch and your other job there, and I strongly suspect the reason you live with your dad is because you have to take care of him."

He stared, his blue eyes darkening to a bruised purple.

"But when you're here, *be* here. You've got nowhere else to be when you're at work. You do such a great job with patients. I've seen it. If you could just...be nice to your coworkers. What makes you so much better than us that you can't sit and enjoy a meal with us? Why won't you laugh when Guy farts doing that beer commercial dance? Why don't you ask us how our weekends were?"

Caz unfolded from his chair, standing to his full height. Bonnie lost her breath—he was so tall and suddenly so *close*. But she went on. "Why can't you just try to fit in? Everyone wants to like you. They have no reason not to, or at least they didn't when you started here. You're making enemies now, and I hate that. This is a family."

"I don't need *family*. I've had—" He looked down at the carving still in his hands. "You can go on being the popular one, the one saying what everyone else wants to hear even when it's not the truth."

Bonnie was so close to him that she could feel the heat from his body, could smell the fresh wood scent he always seemed to carry, even when he wasn't actively whittling. She could feel the desire to touch him in the very ends of her fingertips, and it didn't make sense—nothing made sense when he was right there, right in front of her. Her anger dissipated, leaving her with nothing but a desire she couldn't—and didn't dare—name.

"Why are you out here?" His voice rumbled in his chest.

"I was looking for you," said Bonnie. He was too near, too close. If she took half a step forward... No, she should back up. She should run away.

But Bonnie didn't run away from much. She continued, "I was worried."

That made him smile. Her worry was funny, apparently. "Worried I'd fallen asleep in an inappropriate place?"

Unforgivably, the thought of her own bed popped into her mind. *That* would be an inappropriate place to sleep. "No..."

Slowly, Caz set the half-carved wolf on the table and lifted his hand, touching the side of her cheek. "Worried that I'd forgotten to stay here? That I'd gone home?"

"Maybe something like that."

His thumb rubbed softly against her jawline. "I shouldn't do this," he said, his voice even lower. Darker.

"No," she agreed. But her own hand lifted and pressed his to her cheek. "You shouldn't."

Their eyes, already locked, heated. In that second, Bonnie could see reflected on his face the way she felt—the intensity of her longing swept through her.

She wanted him.

CHAPTER 13

Bonnie couldn't tell who moved first, but the kiss was sudden—explosive—and she lost her breath like she'd fallen out of a tree onto her back. She gasped against his mouth and he made a low groan in his throat. As his tongue plundered hers, as she tasted him, her senses filled with the headiness of the kiss. Caz's arms went around her and his hands went low, cupping her buttocks, pulling her tightly against him. He was hard against her—she could feel exactly what she was doing to him. His lips teased and bit, tugging at hers. The harder she kissed him, the closer her got to her. The more strongly he pulled her against his body, the more she pressed herself against him. She wished she could feel more of his skin, more of his body... *More.*

"Stupid clothes," he muttered.

"I hate them," she agreed, and then his mouth took hers again. Caz bit her bottom lip and then sucked it sweetly as if to make up for it. She dug her short fingernails into the ridge of muscle at the top of his deltoid, and his quick intake of breath didn't stop her from digging in harder.

The lower half of Bonnie's body seemed to be on fire. If

she'd pulled away from him and seen that her uniform shorts were smoking, she wouldn't have been surprised.

Caz pulled away an inch and locked his gaze with hers again. His eyes were even darker now, indigo and midnight. "I want you," he said.

Common sense, Bonnie counseled herself. *Common sense.* She knew she had some. She wasn't exactly sure where it was right now, but she was known for it. Bonnie kept a cool head in the most difficult of settings. That's what she was good at.

Not one single part of her was cool right now.

Not one.

He said it again, "I want you, Bonnie."

The words, all by themselves, had a devastating effect on her. The few remaining muscles in her body which hadn't been trembling started to shake. She wanted to sit, to slip to the ground, but his arms were still around her, and the hard rigidity of his body, of his...of *all* of him steadied her.

"I want you, too," she said.

"But we can't," Caz said.

Disappointment was a sharp blade that cut into her skin, even though she knew he was right. She groaned and drove her hips against his. "Good *grief.* What have we been *doing* then?"

Was that a smile that played at the edges of his lips? Sure enough, his eyes warmed, too, the indigo melting to ultramarine. "I mean we can't do anything here," he said.

"*What good does having a bed at work do me?*" she managed to say through the tightness in her throat. Half of her was kidding, of course. The other half (the lower half) was frighteningly serious.

"A date," he said, and then touched his lips to the sensitive part of her neck just below her earlobe.

"A date?"

"Like the last one. Only better."

She shivered. "Better?"

"Just you. Just me. Dinner. My house."

His broad arm wrapped around her and pulled her harder against him, leaving no doubt in her mind that neither of them were thinking about dinner at his house.

"Okay then."

"Bed."

"What?" Bonnie's thoughts were muddled, her brain melted. "No, I agree, not here…"

"We both still have to sleep." His voice was softer now. Sweet. "We go back to our beds."

"Oh." He was right. "Yeah."

Bonnie stepped back and rubbed her arms, grateful for the night air chilling her skin, cooling her.

"I'll follow you in two minutes," Caz said.

He wasn't touching her anymore, but the way he stood there, the way his chest still rose and fell—she'd done that to him. And he was the reason she felt the way she did now, as if flames were licking at her undercarriage. She was a VW on the highway, burning to its magnesium core. "No," Bonnie said, pressing her hands to her cheeks. "You go first. I'll follow you." She needed another minute to pull herself together and cool herself off.

Or another couple of years.

Caz gave one nod. He didn't kiss her again. He didn't say another word; he just turned on his heel and yanked open the heavy station door.

Bonnie sank down in the chair he'd been occupying when she came out. She reached down and picked up some of the wood shavings at her feet. They were softer than she'd expected, and lighter.

Spilling them from hand to hand, Bonnie breathed. She was sunk. Completely. She had a thing for Caz Lloyd, the stubborn cowboy, the only one of her coworkers she would have voted off the island just a month ago.

Good grief. She touched her lips with a thin shaving. Her skin was tender from the scratch of his stubble.

She had more than just a thing. She was headed down a steep hill on two wheels, speeding up too fast. There was more than a small chance she was going to wreck, head over handlebars.

At least she'd be flying when she went.

CHAPTER 14

Lying in the dorm in the dark, Caz counted the ways he was screwed. One by one, he ran through the reasons he had to break the date *that he'd suggested* like they were bills in the folder on the ranch desk.

Reason Number One: Bonnie was his coworker. He did *not* date coworkers. Ever.

Addendum to Reason Number One: But wasn't there a time for everything? Shouldn't Caz be more flexible? Right? Wasn't that what people were always saying? Besides, it wasn't like they worked that *much* with each other. No more than ten days a month. That wasn't bad.

Caz heard the dorm door's click. Either one of the firefighters had gotten up to use the john or it was Bonnie, coming back to bed. Caz didn't realize he was holding his breath until he heard the soft *shush-shush* of her slippers coming off. He heard the rustle of her sheets being pulled back. His hearing had never been so sharp—he could practically hear her eyelashes blinking.

Reason Number Two: Bonnie was too much *fun*. He

didn't date fun women. Fun women didn't tell you the truth. They lied about their feelings. They lied about what they were going to do, what they wanted to do, what they would do. Caz liked blunt women who verged on rude, the ones who might hurt a guy's feelings, sure, but the ones who told the truth. You always knew where you were with them. They wouldn't run away and never come back.

Addendum to Reason Number Two: Fun was surprisingly, astonishingly sexy.

Caz heard another rustle. Had she just turned over in bed? Was she facing him on the other side of the partition? If the wall weren't there, would she throw her leg over his and lie there, face to face, until he had to kiss her to stop his heart from doing that weird jumping thing it did whenever she was near him?

Reason Number Three: Was it three? He'd lost track somewhere. But he knew what it was. It was the real reason he couldn't actually date Bonnie, the real reason he was an ass for even considering it, and a bigger ass for suggesting it to her. The real reason he couldn't date Bonnie Maddern was that she was too good for him. She deserved more than just a guy who was trying to make it through every day the best he could. She deserved someone who was already put together, not someone who was barely keeping control of the reins. Bonnie didn't know what it was like to wish your own father was dead. A good man didn't wish for that, even if his father was trapped in a hell he couldn't get out of. A good son didn't take a job that kept him away from his own home 48 hours at a time. A good son wasn't *grateful* for mandated overtime.

Addendum to Reason Number Three: Blank. Caz came up blank.

A pillow-thump. That's what that sound was. He knew it because he'd tossed his own pillow around on the bed at least six times since he got under the sheets. Nothing was comfortable. Caz knew what *would* be comfortable, though. Pulling Bonnie's length against his own body as they lay in a bed that was big enough to hold them both, a bed bigger than either of these tiny twin beds they were lying in now, alone…

Heat rushed through him again, the thought of her body making him so hard it actually hurt. He forced himself to lie still. Were her ears straining to hear him the same way his were?

Okay, "comfortable" might not be the first thing that came to mind when he thought about holding her body against his.

Hot. Wet. Gorgeous.

Comfortable was for later, for after, for when she was flushed and spent and happy, resting against his shoulder as their sweat dried under the fan that slowly rotated above his bed.

Caz rolled away from facing the wall.

From facing her.

Asking her out had been a stupid thing to do, almost as stupid as imagining her lying there on the other side of the wall. He bet she was already asleep. He bet Bonnie had barely given him another thought before drifting off into dreams.

At least, he hoped that was true. And he wished for one more thing: that her dreams were sweet.

She deserved that.

He should break the date. Take it back. There were so many reasons…

Then Caz rolled back to face the wall, knowing the very last thing in the world he'd ever do was break the date he'd made with Bonnie.

He pressed his palm flat against the partition and kept it there.

Then he slept.

CHAPTER 15

She arrived in a dress. Standing at the cottage window Caz could see past the big house and down to the driveway. Hot damn if Bonnie Maddern didn't ride up on her bicycle wearing a short red dress.

A lot of people, when they rode bikes, looked as if they were trying to reclaim their youth. Caz suspected he looked that way on his, just a guy trying to be a kid again. But in that red dress, Bonnie looked all woman as she rode up the driveway. He could see the muscles in her legs as she stepped off the bike, and he spent a split second lost in regret that she knew how to dismount without flipping up her skirt accidentally. She'd even worn low heels, some strappy black sandal things that looked sure to get caught in the spokes of a wheel but apparently hadn't. From her rear pannier, she took out a bottle of wine. Wine. At the house. How long had it been since he'd allowed himself a glass when he was home? Being home was so much like being at work—being repeatedly torn from sleep to care for someone who needed his help—that he rarely had even a beer after coming in from the barn.

Empty handed except for the wine bottle, Bonnie approached the front door of the big house.

No. Not there! He'd forgotten to…Caz raced out the front of the cottage, waving a hand and calling to her. "Over here! Bonnie! Here!" Yeah, he sounded like a twelve-year-old with a crush on a girl on the playground. *This* was exactly why he didn't ask women he dated to the ranch. He wouldn't want a woman to meet his father—she'd be freaked out by the vacant stare, the noisy wheezing his father made, the line of drool that often hung to his father's shirt.

Bonnie, though.

She was different.

Caz was by no means going to let himself think about what that actually meant. Neither was he going to let her go into the big house. His cottage was all she needed to see.

"Hi," she said, thrusting the wine at him. "I brought you this."

"Great," he said. Awkwardly, he leaned forward and pecked her on the cheek, much like a cousin would do to another family member. *Awesome.* This was starting out with a bang. Unsexy cousin cheek kiss. Next he'd punch her in the shoulder and offer to let her hold a dead fish.

Bonnie, though, apparently heedless of his tension, walked into the cottage with a quick step—even in those complicated sandals—and didn't seem to notice the awkwardness hanging between them like a pottery wind chime. She went straight to the living room's glass windows and stared out. "You're kidding me," she said.

"What?" Caz looked out and saw what was always out there: the barn, the fields, a few horses, some sheep.

"You get to *look* at this? Every day?" When her gaze met his, her dark rosewood eyes were shining.

"Look at that," she said. "It's like something from a

movie. The sheep, all idyllic and cute, and the horses, like you're about to ride one."

"I might. You never know."

"And the barn. A red barn! Why are so many barns red?"

"Hundreds of years ago, farmers in Europe mixed linseed with milk and ferrous oxide to treat the wood."

Bonnie stared at him. "I didn't think you'd have an answer for that."

He shrugged. "I know about wood."

Bonnie blinked. "Must be nice to be able to see home from far away."

Danged if she wasn't right. More times than he could count, he'd come over Pine Bluff to spot the barn with relief.

Bonnie said, "You know what I look at every day from my living room?"

"No." Suddenly, Caz very much wanted to know.

"I look at my super-overgrown lawn. My old lawn-mower cost me twenty-five bucks at a yard sale, and it takes two hundred pulls to get it started. I don't always have the patience."

"Two hundred?" Was her penchant for exaggeration alarming or cute? He couldn't decide.

She nodded firmly. "At *least*. Also from my window, I get to look at Mr. Cavanaugh's old tighty-whities as he goes outside to get the paper. The good news is they're not tight anymore. The bad news is they're not white, either."

"Your neighbor goes outside in his underwear?"

She nodded again, and then he watched the way the western sun lit the top of her blond hair till it shone gold. "I have this working theory that he's a nudist, but he's also very shy. I think when he's inside his house he never wears any clothes at all. His underpants are just the bare minimum to stay legal outside."

"What does he wear when he goes to the grocery store?"

"He gets Amazon deliveries. For everything. He might be eating cheap dog food for all I know. I've only ever seen him leave the house to get the paper off the lawn."

Caz wanted to listen to her talk all night. About anything. Just as long as she kept smiling at him like that. "What about taking out the trash?"

"Done in the dead of night. I've never seen him roll a can in or out. They almost seem to move by themselves." She dropped a cheeky wink at him, and Caz realized that he'd do just about anything for another one of those.

He cleared his throat. "So, I made steak."

"You did? Already?"

"I haven't cooked it yet." Caz felt awkward again.

"Ah."

"But I'm going to," he clarified.

"I'd like that. While I'll eat a steak pretty rare, it has to at least kiss the fire once."

Kiss the fire. Instantly, he was distracted again. Yep, her lips were still the same, still full and sweet-looking, exactly the kind of lips any man would want to taste. And Caz would lay good money that if he kissed them again, he'd be the one on fire.

Why had he asked her here? Just so he could kiss her again?

"So." Caz felt stupid and slow. Something about Bonnie made his blood feel thick. This date was doomed.

"So," Bonnie said, turning so that she faced him. "When do I get to meet your dad?"

An alert shot through him like an electric buzzer wired to his spine. "How about never?"

"What? No way. That's why I'm here."

Caz thought she was here because when they kissed, the whole world went up in flames that neither of them could seem to put out. "You're here for my good cooking."

"I can get that at my mom's house. I want to meet your dad."

"Your own dad isn't a cranky enough bastard for you?"

Bonnie's smile was like sunshine breaking through clouds. "My dad? He's the eternal optimist. Never has a bad thing to say about anyone. Ever. If you want cranky, you need to see my mother before her first three cups of coffee."

"So that's where you get that from."

"What are you talking about?"

"You can't even see straight before you have your coffee."

"*Moi?*" Bonnie stuck her thumb into her chest. "You must be joking. I'm Mary Sunshine when I wake up."

"If Mary Sunshine is stuck in a thunderstorm."

"I'm sweetness and light."

"You're bitter and dark, just the way you like your coffee."

Bonnie looked surprised. "You know how I take my coffee?"

"Yeah," he said. *Whoops.*

"I don't know how you drink yours."

"That's because you're a jerk," he said lightly.

Bonnie laughed. "Wait. You don't drink it."

"Why do you say that?"

"I know how everyone takes theirs. Guy takes three million spoons of sugar and little to no coffee. Hank is milk, no sugar. Tox is a splash of cream. You don't drink coffee at all."

Caz looked out the window. A low beam of late sunlight was warming the barn's roof. "Never needed it."

"You just wake up elated with life? With that cheerful disposition we all know and love?"

The last word fell from her lips into the room as if she'd dropped a book flat to the floor. *Love.* Her cheeks went pink. Caz felt all logic leave his head. There was one thing, and one thing only, that he wanted to do at that moment, and it involved a lot of his skin on hers, and very little to do with cooking steak on the back grill.

"Your dad," she said, finally breaking the sudden electric tension between them.

"Yeah. Okay." Caz shook his head. "But don't say I didn't warn you."

CHAPTER 16

Caz's dad Tony was pretty bad off. Bonnie wasn't shocked—by the way Caz had prepped her, she'd only have been shocked if they'd gone in the room and found a dead man—but she was taken aback by the blankness of Tony's stare.

"Hey, Joyce," said Caz to the small woman who was reading a book in the chair next to the window. "This is Bonnie."

"Oh, goodness," said Joyce, standing. Her hands fluttered to her short hair, patting it down. "Caz said someone was coming by, but I just assumed... Oh, it's so nice to meet you."

Bonnie wondered what Joyce had assumed. Did Caz often have women over? Was there a certain one Joyce was expecting? No one had ever said Caz was single—she'd just assumed that he was by the fact that he kissed like a man who was born to kiss her. Maybe she shouldn't have put so much stock in that assumption.

"Is he going to cook for you?"

Caz nodded. "Just steak."

"Oh, you're in for a treat. His grilling is the best in the whole world."

Bonnie had the feeling Joyce would have said that if he were making her twice-warmed concrete for dinner.

"But you want to visit with Tony. I'll just go and put the washing in...it was nice meeting you, dear." Joyce drifted tactfully out the door. Then she popped her head back around, as if she couldn't help it. "Oh, it is *so* nice to meet you. *So* nice. Caz finally bringing a girl to the house. Oh!"

Caz made a noise that could only be called a groan. Bonnie swallowed her amusement and focused on the man in the bed.

He was tiny. Bonnie could tell he'd been a big man—his legs and arms were long under the light sheet, like Caz's were, and the skin at the sides of his face, near his ears, was loose, as if it had once fit around a larger person. His eyes were open, staring at the ceiling, and he hadn't looked at them since they'd entered the room. He made a chewing motion with his mouth, and when he smacked his lips open and closed, Bonnie could see that he'd lost his teeth.

"He can't wear his dentures anymore," was all Caz said.

"Will you introduce me?"

Caz's eyes narrowed as he looked at her, as if to weigh whether or not she was serious. "He's not very with it. As you can see."

Bonnie raised her eyebrows. She waited. Politely.

Caz moved forward and touched his father on the shoulder. "Dad, this is Bonnie Maddern. She's here to meet you." His voice was gruffer than the voice he normally used on patients at work, but Bonnie could see his touch was gentle. Carefully, Caz straightened the collar of his father's pajamas. "He was always vain about his appearance. I know he'd hate this..." His voice trailed off.

Bonnie stepped forward and put her hand over Tony's wrinkled one. His hand had been plucking at the sheet fitfully, but it stilled as she touched him. "Mr. Lloyd, it's such a pleasure to meet you."

Caz pulled up the sheet a little higher and then moved to take the blanket from the foot of the bed. Bonnie helped, unfolding it on her side, bringing it up so they could tuck it under his arms.

"It's okay," said Caz, as if she'd complained. "He doesn't know what's going on. He's in the last stages and—"

Bonnie put her finger over her lips. "*Shhh.*" In a louder voice she said, "So this is the amazing father you told me about."

Caz shot a look at her that seemed more made of confusion than anything else.

"And you're right. He is handsome." Bonnie tilted her head. "No, not more handsome than you are, Caz, I think you're wrong there. I think you're both equally good looking."

Caz made a choking sound as Bonnie winked at him.

"Mr. Lloyd, I work with your son at the Darling Bay Fire Department. I can tell you this, we sure were lucky to get him. I'm friends with one of the people in HR, and she says that he was not only the most competent applicant, but he was the most eager to work with us. She told me that he had family in the area he wanted to be near, and now I see why. With a place like this, I can totally imagine why he'd want to be home. You've built a beautiful house on an amazing spread of land." Bonnie scanned the bed to make sure she wasn't going to hurt him or sit on his oxygen tube, and then she perched on the edge. "You don't mind, do you? I rode all the way here on my bicycle, and it's a good ten miles. Of course, you probably know exactly how far it is to town from here, don't you? Caz told me you know every inch of this ranch like the back of your hand. My family, we don't have anything like this. Do you know my parents? You might, if you ever shopped for knick knacks in the antique section of downtown. My mother owns Darling Bay Trinkets, and if you've ever been to her shop, I guarantee you'd remember her. Very few people forget her."

"Kind of like you," said Caz quietly.

Bonnie looked at him as he leaned against an old, dark bureau. He'd been watching as she talked, his crystalline eyes intently focused on her.

Caz spoke again. "You're lying to him."

"I'm not."

He arched an eyebrow. "Good looking?"

Bonnie felt color heat her cheeks and she lowered her voice to a whisper even though it felt rude to do so in Tony Lloyd's presence. "I think he is. Look at those high cheekbones." She spoke directly to Tony then. "Don't listen to him. You've had a better shave today than your son has. He's all stubble, but I can tell you're a man who's always taken care of himself."

"He was," said Caz in a low voice. "He really was. Can you..."

"What?"

Caz looked at the ground and then met her eyes directly. "I hate lies."

"Caz, I'm not—"

"But can you keep talking to him like that for a little while longer?"

Bonnie blinked in confusion. "Okay?"

"It sounds...nice."

"Okay, then."

Caz took a hesitant step forward and then, confusingly,

he folded his arms and pressed his back against the bureau again. He nodded, as if to give her permission.

Bonnie smiled. She might not know much about what to do with Caz, who sent windmills whirling in her stomach and made her ache in a way she didn't understand, but she knew how to talk to a man locked inside his own body, a man who'd barely moved since they'd entered the room.

She scooted an inch sideways so she was more firmly planted on the bed. "I hope you don't mind me sitting here with you, sir. Your son Caz is...I've...enjoyed getting to know him a little better. I told him just the other day that a man with such a big personality like his had to have had a strong father at home." She'd said no such thing. "I know you don't feel like talking right now. If that changes, you just let me know, okay? In the meantime, I'll just tell you a little bit about my family. My maternal grandmother—maybe you knew her? Hazel Lake? She was a good woman. And the way she ended up in Darling Bay involved a pig in a wheelbarrow, if you can believe that..."

CHAPTER 17

Caz watched.

He listened.

Bonnie spun a tale about a baby pig that fell out of a wheelbarrow on a road her grandmother was bicycling (maybe two wheels ran in the blood). The story included a dinghy that sank, and a man with silver eyes who saved her grandmother from drowning, and something about a lightning storm and a bag of oranges, or maybe it was lemons. Caz felt as if maybe he were the one with Alzheimer's. He couldn't remember where the story was going or why she was telling it. But when she said, a light lilt in her voice, "Can you believe it? A moth that blocked the whole moon!" he felt his mouth curve into a smile.

More incredible than the story, though, was the fact that Tony Lloyd opened his eyes. He looked right at the blonde sitting on the edge of his bed, his eyes focusing on her as if he saw her. As if he recognized her.

And then, miracle of all miracles, he *smiled* at her.

Taking care of an Alzheimer's patient at this stage often felt like taking care of a baby. There wasn't much rhyme or reason to any of the sounds they made. They couldn't control their limbs or their bodily functions. Their smiles could just as easily be gas.

But the smile on his father's face now was his father's old smile, the one he reserved for when he was happy with a horse's recovery, or when he laid down a full house.

Tony *smiled* at Bonnie. He always had liked blondes.

Bonnie smiled back, and it struck a low bell inside Caz, a tone that rang through his entire frame. A tone he recognized, somehow.

Bonnie took his father's hand, pressing it between her own. She leaned forward and said, "Well, hello there, handsome. You're going to be just fine, aren't you?"

Something lit in Caz's father's eyes. Something he hadn't seen in a long time. Was it...hope? That couldn't be... she shouldn't...

Bonnie said it again, "You're going to be fine. A strong man like you, I see where Caz gets it from. Now I'm going to tell you the rest of the story, okay?"

She kept spinning her tale of runaway pigs and red bicycles, and within a few minutes, his father was snoring softly, the way he did most of the day now.

Joyce put her head around the corner, and her eyes lit with surprise to see Bonnie on the bed. "Oh! Isn't this something? You put him to sleep for me?"

Bonnie's tale over, she slid sideways, careful to stand up from the bed without jostling Tony. "I'm so glad I met you," she whispered touching Tony's cheek with the back of her fingers.

Something inside Caz splintered, something he wasn't sure he'd be able to sand away or fix with wood glue.

The thing was, Caz could tell she really *was* glad. She was happy she'd just spent thirty minutes with a man who only looked at her once. And even though she'd done her usual lying to a patient (*You'll be fine, you'll be great*), instead of being angry with her, his chest felt expansive. Grateful. Warm.

The very *least* he could do was cook for her.

He took her hand, ignoring her look of surprise. He led her through the house, out the back door and across the grassy area between the two houses. The sunset, red and orange at its heart, was starting to pale to coral on the edges.

Bonnie stopped, putting her head back. "Look at that view. You can't see the ocean from here, but it doesn't matter much, does it?"

"Incredible," Caz said. He wasn't looking at the sky.

In the kitchen of the cottage, he said, "Sit," pointing at the barstool on the opposite side of a wooden island he'd built the winter the old maple came down. What was that, four years ago now? That had been the first Christmas he'd known something was really wrong with his father, the first time he thought he might have to move home. "Wine?"

"Sure," she said. "What can I help with?"

"You can just sit there. You've done enough." He straightened from reaching for the bottle opener. "You've done..." His brain whirred and stalled. He didn't have the words he wanted. "You're..."

"Bossy? Pushy? Annoying? I've heard all those this week, and that was only from my mother."

"Amazing."

Bonnie went all pink again. Caz loved it.

It was so *different* for her.

In a crisis, she was calm. Her head was in just the right place. Last week, when the seventeen-year-old skateboarder had landed in the gutter, giving himself a double compound fracture, she'd never paused chatting to the kid while they loaded him. She was able to treat and talk at the same time, all the while calming a kid who was almost out of his mind from shock and pain. Right now, though? She looked totally flummoxed, as if he'd gotten her drunk and then asked her to solve word problems with a pen and no calculator.

He worked fast. It was a simple dinner, the kind he made himself all the time. He led her outside to the deck and while she sat on the porch swing, he grilled the steak. He threw together a quick green salad, and brought out some bread and butter fresh from the Johnson's dairy down the road. He added salt and pepper to the small table on the edge of the deck and brought out two cloth napkins, just to cover all his bases. Almost full dark, he added a brass camping lantern that gave a low, companionable hiss.

"Fancy," she said, holding up her napkin to the yellow light. "The embroidered flowers are sweet. My mother would love these. Do you know who did it?"

He cleared his throat. "My dad."

"Really?"

"My mom split on us. He kind of took on everything. Some things he was better at than others. He would sew—embroider, I guess—in the evenings while we watched TV. Said it relaxed him. I think it helped wreck his eyes, but I will say that it was one of his last skills to go. He lost the motor skills to undo his own pants, but he could still stitch a flower like it was a contest."

"Do *you* embroider?" Her voice was a flirt. A tease. He wanted to cup his hand around the back of her neck and draw her in for a kiss that was hard and deep.

Caz paused. He wasn't a good liar.

"You do," she guessed.

He sawed at the edge of the steak he'd charred a bit too

much. "I wanted to be just like my dad. What's a kid gonna do?"

"That's the most adorable thing I ever heard."

Caz mock-glared at her. "I'm not adorable. I'm tough."

"Sure. Embroiderer."

"I build houses." He held up his hands. "With these."

He expected her to laugh, but instead she said earnestly, like she wanted to know, "Really? How?"

"How?" he repeated.

"Like, from scratch? Or do you mean you hire someone and then you help? Or do you just paint at the end?"

Caz felt warmth spread through him. "From scratch. We built most of this place, my dad and me. And...my cabin up north is almost done."

"Everything," she clarified. "Like, you put in the windows and the countertops? The electricity, too?"

"Yep. I did everything myself, with some help from a couple of guys when I needed manpower with things that were too heavy for just one person."

Bonnie cupped her chin in her hands. "You love it. That's why you whittle all the time."

He shrugged. "I guess."

"When will you finish the cabin?"

The skin on his arms felt chilled. "When I can."

"Your dad."

Caz tried to smile. "A lot depends." Who was this woman who made him talk? Who made him tell her the important things? Why did he want to tell her more? Why did he want to tell her everything? He wanted to explain the beams that ran under this cottage, and he wanted to tell her the dream he'd had about her the night before, the one he could barely remember now, except that it had warmed him to his fingertips. "So," he said. "You gonna tell the guys?"

"About what?"

"The embroidery."

Bonnie grinned. "Of course I am."

"You wouldn't."

"How are you going to stop me?"

It was a challenge. A direct one. There was nothing for him to do but stand and walk the two short steps around the small table. Bonnie looked up at him, and the question in her eyes was gratifyingly replaced by understanding. He sunk his fingers into the back of her hair and leaned down, kissing her the way he'd wanted to since she first skidded her bike to that short, quick stop in front of the house.

It was, perhaps, the only thing he'd ever wanted to do. Maybe the thing he was born to do.

Her hand wrapped around his wrist and gripped him so tightly it almost hurt. He wanted her to touch him like that everywhere. She stood, sliding her body along the length of his, never breaking the kiss. Her lips were hot and sweet, and he dimly heard her fork clatter to the deck at their feet. Dinner was forgotten. Nothing mattered but the way her tongue slid against his, the way her breathing speeded up, the way he could feel her pulse racing when his fingers feathered her throat. His heart was beating just as fast, juddering under his shirt.

Caz sucked her bottom lip lightly. Her arm wrapped around his neck and he felt her small breasts push against his chest. "Caz."

"Mad."

There was no annoyance in her eyes at the nickname, just the fire of desire. "Take me to bed," she said.

"But," he said, raking his teeth against the soft skin at

her jaw and then sliding his tongue up to her ear. "What about dessert?"

"What kind of dessert?" she said, her lips finding his again.

Against her mouth, he said, "Strawberry shortcake. First berries of the season."

She dug her fingernails into the skin of his arms as his tongue teased its way down toward the soft hollow at the base of her throat. Her scent, peaches and soap, was intoxicating, making him feel weightless and almost dizzy. He kissed his way back to her mouth just as she said, "Whipped cream?"

Two words had never been sexier, he decided. "Naturally."

"You'd better bring it to bed with us. Just in case."

He laughed out loud, the sound of his happiness soaring to meet the starlight overhead.

CHAPTER 18

Bonnie's grandmother used to knit everywhere she went. She stuck the sock she was always working on into whatever purse or bag was handiest, the ball of yarn inevitably getting tangled in among the pens and Tylenol bottles and individually wrapped Life Savers. Bonnie was the most accomplished at untangling the mess, and they spent hours together, tracking where the yarn's tail went, tracing the ball along its path.

When Bonnie woke in Caz's arms, she felt like that ball of yarn. If she drew her arm from under his side, then she'd have to extricate her leg which was pinned somehow between him and the wall. Her hair was stuck under his pillow and his other arm was clamped firmly around her.

She'd never felt safer in her whole life. Not that she spent a lot of time feeling unsafe—she knew how to take care of herself. She'd never minded sleeping alone. In fact, she loved waking and rolling over in her big bed at home, splaying her arms and legs, letting her feet hang over the end, with no one in her way. She never gave herself a cramp being stuck in one position when she slept alone.

That said, muscle cramps and all, this was better. Somehow, even as uncomfortable as she was, this was better than being comfortable in her own spacious (and very empty) bed.

"Hi," Caz said into her hair.

She jumped. "Holy crap."

A low laugh was all she heard, his chest rumbling. As his arms tightened around her, she shimmied in closer. "How long have you been awake?" she asked.

"Just long enough to…" A pause. "For me to feel happy."

Bonnie felt something melt inside her, right around her knees. "Oh."

Caz took her hand and held it in the air with his own. "Look how small your hand is." He compared them over their heads, pressing his fingers along hers.

"I have my mother's hands. And my father's feet. Long toes."

Another rumble of laughter. "I bet I like those toes, too, but your hand doesn't require me to move to inspect."

He could inspect just about anything right now and Bonnie wouldn't mind. The warmth of him was keeping her drowsy, even though small flutters of excitement shot through her as he twined his fingers again with hers.

"You were good last night," Caz said.

She blinked and grinned. "Well, thank you."

He kissed the tip of her thumb. "No, well, yeah, but I mean with my dad. The way you talked to him."

"Oh. Of course." She loved the warmth that pooled through her.

"Did you know you talk in your sleep?"

"Uh-oh."

"Uh-huh."

"What did I say?"

His lips pressed against her temple. "It didn't make much sense. Something about Caz and a pig in a wheelbarrow. Oh, and how you just had the best sex you've ever had in your life."

"Well, that makes sense."

Caz drew back, that slow, sexy smile wide on his mouth. "I'm just teasing."

"I wasn't."

"Sugar, you don't have to flatter me."

"I'm not." She stretched, reaching her arms over her head and pressing her fingertips to the headboard. "It's the first time I've ever had sex at all. So of course it was the best."

Bonnie felt Caz still, his muscles going rigid.

"You're not serious."

She felt a giggle rise in her chest, but she kept her face still and opened her eyes wide. She blinked once, slowly, keeping her gaze on his. "Should I have told you?"

Caz made a small sputtering sound. "Your first time? That was your first time?" His arms tightened around her, and she was in the biggest bear hug of her life. "Sugar. Oh, love, did I hurt you? You should have told me."

The word *love* sent a shiver through her, and for the life of her, Bonnie couldn't tell what kind of shiver it was. She'd only been teasing. A silly joke, that's all it had been. "Okay, maybe it wasn't my *first* time." She gave a grin, hoping he'd guffaw and match it.

But he didn't.

"Wait. So it wasn't your first...I'm confused."

"Kidding! I'm thirty-one, come on." Bonnie shouldn't press the joke, she knew she shouldn't, but she couldn't help teasing him a little more. "I can't believe you fell for that. That's hilarious."

Caz shot backward. From being enveloped by him, to being alone on her side of the bed in mere seconds. "It's what?"

Bonnie scooted to get closer to him again, her skin suddenly chilled. "I was teasing."

"Why would you...? That's..." His face darkened, his eyebrows drawing together. "That doesn't make any sense."

Worry crept along her bare arms, colder than the chill. "Caz."

"I don't get how that's a joke. Do you *ever* say anything you actually mean?"

"That's not fair—"

"Nothing you said to my dad was true last night. And I fell for it." He shook his head as if to clear it. "Nothing you say at the firehouse ever means anything. It's all joking with you. Even with patients. When they're scared, you just brush them off."

It was Bonnie's turn to draw back. "What?"

"You don't listen. Maybe you don't listen to anyone."

She felt herself wince. "It was just a *joke*."

"Come on, Bonnie." Caz stood, standing naked without shame in front of her. She could almost see the heat rising from him, and it wasn't desire or lust like it had been last night. The night before, his hands had been wide and strong, giving her nothing but pleasure. His mouth had been firm and insistent, teasing her to heights she truly had never known before. *That* would have been the thing to tell him. That's what she should have said. She shouldn't have made a stupid crack about her virginity. It *wasn't* funny. She got that.

Now his hands were tight at his side, and she could see the strain in the muscle that jumped in the side of his jaw.

His mouth was a hard line, no sign of the man who'd made her moan in the dark.

"I'm sorry?"

Caz lifted one eyebrow. "That's it? A question?"

Bonnie scrambled into a sitting position, wrapping the sheet around her as she went. It was still tucked in at the bottom of the bed, though she wasn't sure how that was possible, given the way they'd swum through the sheets the night before. She wasn't as easily confident in her body, not like he was. She couldn't just sit unclothed with Caz Lloyd, in his house, while he watched her with those angry eyes. "No. Not a question. I'm sorry. I thought it would make you laugh."

His voice was softer, but he was still far away. "It wasn't funny. If it had been your first time, I would have been different with you. Slower. More gentle."

She tried a smile. "You were gentle the third time."

Caz didn't smile back. "You made me think I'd hurt you."

Shaking her head, Bonnie held out her hand in the hope that he would take it. "You didn't. You were perfect."

Her hand just hung there between them. He didn't take it. "You can't just lie to take the pressure off something."

"Hang on a sec, buddy." *He wasn't her buddy—not that...* "You can't call a joke a lie."

"Yes, I can. And I do." He stepped into his jeans, yanking them up unceremoniously. Then he tugged on a light blue T-shirt that made his eyes seem even icier. "Tell me how you feel about me."

Oh, no. She had no idea how she felt about him. Not a clue.

"Come on, you're overreacting," she said, knowing she probably shouldn't. But he was. It wasn't a big deal. She'd teased him, and he hadn't liked it. She'd try not to do it again. That was all he could ask for, wasn't it?

"You don't even know, do you? Do you ever have *any* honest emotions?"

It felt like a slap. "What?"

"I saw your face the other day, with the ducks."

The *ducks?* He was going to bring them into this?

"You were upset. And the one thing you wouldn't do was show it."

Bonnie swung her shoulders in small circles, suddenly feeling the tension she was carrying in them. "I was totally fine."

She hadn't been fine, not even a little. They'd had a call of ducklings in a drain. The engine had been assigned, but she and Caz had been in the area, and they took the call. Ducks stuck in storm drains were common in the spring. They had a special long-handled net they kept folded under the jump seat just for that purpose. Caz had chased the mama duck across the street and over to the pond in Murray Park. Using the net to encourage them, Bonnie had herded the six ducklings across the busy street while Caz blocked it for her. With soft little plops and happy chirps, the babies had followed mama into the pond. A happy ending. Two couples and three families out for a walk stopped to watch. Two of the parents filmed their kids watching the ducks. Everyone was laughing.

Then a little girl shrieked. "It's gone! Something took it! Mommy!"

They all followed her pointing finger. More children's screams followed as, one by one, the ducklings were grabbed and swallowed by the giant koi that Darling Bay City Hall was so proud of.

It had been terrible. Bonnie herself had wanted to

scream. She'd picked up two rocks and then stood there juggling them awkwardly in her hands while the parents' eyes begged her and Caz to do *something*, anything, to stop the carnage. She couldn't throw the rocks—they'd just hit the ducklings. They couldn't go in the water—the ducklings would panic and bolt. The mama duck swam frantically, quacking her alarm, as—one by one—all her babies were taken.

Then they'd had been dispatched to standby at a possible trench rescue (it hadn't been one—just a guy who trapped his leg while digging in his backyard) and they'd had to drive away from the crying children and aghast parents. Bonnie's hands had been shaking, and she'd been glad Caz was driving. She'd felt daggers behind her fore-head, pain that might have been tears, pain she would never admit to. Over *ducks*, of all things. Three CPR failures in a row, she felt fine. But ducks, apparently, broke her.

At the station, she'd popped three Excedrin Migraine and then made "Why did the duck cross the road?" jokes while she made chicken Marsala that night. She felt the headache throb as she cut the meat.

Now, Caz just stared, his arms rigid at his sides. "I understand pushing back the feelings we have about people. If we felt everything normal people feel in our job, we'd go crazy."

It was true. That's why she didn't.

He went on. "But you almost melted down after the ducks. Your voice shook for an hour afterward. I bet you didn't know that."

She hadn't. "I was—"

"That night, in bed, you had a nightmare, do you remember that?"

"No, I didn't."

"You were crying."

"I was *not*." Over ducks? Her? Really?

Caz rolled his eyes. "I was an inch away from you on the other side of the partition. I could hear you." He looked down and then back up. "I thought about going to you, but you stopped as fast as you started, and then your breathing was deep again."

So intimate, to know each other's sleep this well. It was almost more intimate than the mostly not-sleeping they'd done the night before. "I don't remember that," she said. She did, though, remember the raging headache she'd woken with the next morning, and the way her eyes had been puffy. She'd thought it was odd, and she'd taken a few more Excedrin and pushed it out of her mind.

"I know you don't remember. It was a feeling, that's why."

"I'm not a robot. And *you're* one to talk. You don't tell anyone anything. You're lecturing *me* about being honest?"

"Oh, honey," he said, his voice low and rough, rocks on gravel. "I'm always honest. You think those things I said last night weren't true?"

He'd called her gorgeous, intoxicating, sexy as hell, and then, this morning, he'd called her *love*. "I—I don't know."

"How do you feel about me?"

Only one word pulsed in her brain, but it was out of reach of her mouth. "I...think you're...super fun." Good grief.

"I was falling in love with you."

Was.

Caz continued. "But you can't even admit you like me."

"Isn't it *obvious*?" What she'd done last night, the way she'd kissed him—did she really have to attach words to that?

"Nope. Use your words, Mad. Tell me something I don't know. Tell me something I want to know." There was something under his voice, a wish that Bonnie could hear, could almost feel, as if he'd held it out to her to take. His voice softened. "Come on, Mad."

She opened her mouth.

The words didn't come.

Bonnie could almost see him lose his patience. He'd held onto it, and just like that, he let it go.

No. More than that. He let *her* go. She could see it—she wanted to stop it, but it would be like holding back the tide that rushed up every night, drowning the legs of the Darling Bay pier.

"I'm going to go next door and check on my father."

Bonnie scooted backward until her back was pressed against the headboard. Her voice was small. "I'll wait here."

Caz's voice was soft. "Nah. That's okay."

Shock knifed her. "But—"

His hand moved slightly as if he were going to try to touch her, but he was still feet away and he made no effort to get closer. "Bonnie—it's probably better this way."

What way? What *way* was he talking about? Leaving her naked in his bed? Alone? "You're kicking me out?"

"No. You can stay as long as you want."

But he wasn't coming back to bed, to her. He was going to check on his father, and then he'd stay with him. In the other house. She could see that.

Caz open the door. He gave one glance over his shoulder. His eyes were ravaged. Had she done that? Just by making a joke? But inside, she knew it was bigger than that. He'd asked for her honesty. Truth. It was what mattered most to him—that she be able to tell him how she felt.

And then she hadn't. She couldn't.

The door shut softly behind him.

CHAPTER 19

Kicked out. She'd been kicked *out*.

She'd had sex with Caz, a man she hadn't even planned on liking. She'd actively *dis*liked him, in fact. Where had that gone? When had she become the bad guy?

And then he'd kicked her all the way out of his house.

Somewhere, this must have been covered in Miss Manners, wasn't it? Dear Miss Manners, A man made love to me six ways to Sunday and then, in the morning, he asked me to go home. Should I be offended? Thank you, Confused in Darling Bay

Answer: Dear CIDB, You raise an interesting point. But it sounds like there's something you left out, so in this letter I'll leave out the answer and see how you like it.

Dang.

Bonnie locked her bike to the rack she'd insisted her mother install outside Darling Trinkets. The rack was steel painted gold, shaped in the form of a bicycle. Only her mother could find a twee bike rack.

The shop bell tinkled overhead as she entered, and she

heard her mother call, "I'll be right with you! Just dusting a few crystal bowls!" That was code for taking off her flip-flops and slipping on her pretty-but-not-comfortable heels she wore in the store. She thought people (especially older men with money who liked anything Civil War era or older) preferred her to look old-school feminine. Bonnie had seen the way men put cash on the counter for whatever she told them might (or might not have) come from a tobacco plantation in Virginia, and thought her mother might be right about her theory.

"It's just me," Bonnie called. "Just your daughter."

"*Just* my daughter?" Marge came around the corner, one flip-flop on, the other foot barefoot, her arms open. "What could be better?"

Her mother hugged her tight.

That was normal. That's what her mother did.

What Bonnie did wasn't normal.

She burst into tears.

AN HOUR LATER, she'd managed to stem the waterworks to an occasional sniffle. She hadn't been able to tell her mother what had happened. Bonnie and her mother didn't talk about sex, and they *certainly* didn't talk about what happened afterward. Marge didn't even ask, and for that Bonnie was grateful. She couldn't have put it into words. (What would she say? She joked about being a virgin and that's what brought this all on? She knew that wasn't it. She knew in her heart that she'd blown it with Caz by not showing him *herself*. Maybe that part of her was broken. And the fact that she'd lost him—something she'd thought wouldn't matter at all—hurt so deeply, she wondered if she'd pulled something internally. Somewhere near her heart.)

But her mother knew—in the way her mother had always known—exactly what she needed. She tucked Bonnie up in the back of the shop, behind the huge walnut desk, in Bonnie's favorite deep chair. She wrapped her in an afghan that smelled faintly of mothballs and the cinnamon candles that sat in a box nearby. She put a glass of water near her, and a placed the latest *People* magazine on her lap.

The bell jingled and Marge started to slip off her flip-flops to put on her heels. "Oh, honey. Do you want me to go put up the closed sign? I will."

"No, go. Go. I'm fine."

"Oh, Bonnie. My bright shining star." Her mother smiled at her, and Bonnie had a sudden, vivid memory of the day Gramma had died. Bonnie, at almost eighteen, had been inconsolable. It was her first loss, her first experience with death.

Bonnie had been the one to find her. She'd gotten up early, as she usually did, and she'd made them tea. It had been their tradition, all through Bonnie's high school years. Bonnie's mother liked to sleep in, getting up and racing through a shower only an hour before she had to open the store at ten. But Gramma Honor, since she'd moved into the back room after a bad fall, had taught Bonnie what was fun about getting up early. Tea, for one. Gramma Honor would hold the cup in her hands, breathing in the steam. Then she'd sip and say, "Can you feel it? The caffeine? Wait for it. I know you hate waking up early, but here it comes. Burns cleaner than a coffee rush. Just you wait, my bright shining star of a granddaughter."

Then Gramma Honor and Bonnie would make bets about what Bonnie's father would forget when he left the house (always something—a hat, his wallet, his keys), and her grandmother almost always won the bets and loved crowing about it even more than winning the nickels Bonnie had to fork over out of her allowance. Her grandmother made getting up early into something exciting and fun, every day.

That terrible morning, there had been no warning. Of course, Bonnie had thought about losing her grandmother at some point in the future, but it wasn't a real thing to worry about. It wouldn't—it *couldn't*—happen for years and years, not until Bonnie was old enough to know how to handle it. Gramma Honor was strong, anyway. Besides that fall and the broken clavicle that went with it, her health couldn't have been better. She had the blood pressure of a forty-year-old and the cholesterol of a runner.

So there had been nothing to prepare Bonnie for opening her grandmother's door, tray in hand, to find nothing in Gramma's bed but the shell of the person she'd loved.

Bonnie had dropped the tray, breaking both tea cups, burning her feet with the scalding liquid.

She'd known.

Funny, she'd hadn't exactly known *what* she'd known. If she'd been asked, she wouldn't have said Gramma Honor was dead. But she knew the woman she loved wasn't in that room.

Without remembering moving, she'd found herself in her mother's darkened bedroom. "Mom. Mama, wake up." She hadn't called her mother that since she was eight and broke her arm in a fall off her rollerblades. "Mama, come."

In her grandmother's room, Bonnie's mother had touched Honor's cheek, felt her cold skin.

"What do we do?" whispered Bonnie. There had to be something to do.

Marge sighed and sat on the edge of the bed, keeping one hand on Gramma Honor's lower leg. "Nothing, honey."

"CPR."

"I don't think so."

"No, we have to *try*." Bonnie pushed past her mother's legs and started tugging on her grandmother's shoulders. "We learned it in P.E. We have to get her on the floor."

"Bonnie." Her mother tried to still Bonnie's hands.

"We have to *do* something."

"Honey." Her mother's voice broke. "She's gone. She's cold. Look, her hands are still. We can't—we can't get her back."

"But there's nothing *wrong* with her." There wasn't, except that she wasn't breathing. Gramma was healthy. On her old ten-speed, just last year, at eighty-seven, Bonnie's grandmother had almost managed to pass her on the way the strawberry stand. "She's healthy. There's nothing *wrong* with her."

There was, though. There was one thing wrong. Her grandmother had left the room. Without Bonnie, without asking permission, without saying goodbye, Gramma Honor had left her.

Bonnie had felt her eyes fill with tears. "No."

"Don't cry," said her mother.

Don't *cry*? When there was nothing else to do? Anger had filled Bonnie. "If I'd gotten up earlier, I could have *saved* her. It's my fault."

Her mother had grabbed her then, hard, pulling her to

her chest in a hug so tight Bonnie lost her breath. "Don't you ever say that again. It's not your fault. Do *not* say that again. You were the brightest part of her life. She called you her star for a reason. You're the brightest part of *my* life. Keep being that, my love. Keep shining bright. No tears, just be strong. I need you now."

Her mother said that over and over that terrible week. *I need you now.* Bonnie, at almost-eighteen, had taken her job seriously. She hadn't gone to school, even though it meant missing the last week of her senior year. While everyone else ditched school to go to the senior picnic, Bonnie had been working with the funeral home. While her friends took the long school bus ride to grad night at Disneyland, Bonnie had been ordering the flowers, putting the obituary in the paper. Under her watchful gaze, her mother fell apart. Her father made it his full-time job to take care of her mother, leaving everything else to Bonnie.

And she'd risen to the occasion. The only time she'd felt completely helpless was at the funeral itself, when she'd gotten up to say a few words. There, in front of the microphone, she'd only said, "My grandmother—" before her voice clogged with tears. She couldn't speak around them. She'd felt nothing but helplessness and anger. Her father had walked up the few steps to the podium to help her, but Bonnie had stubbornly shaken her head until she could swallow hard enough to finally push back the tears. Then she'd been able to speak about Gramma Honor.

Her mother was right. It was better not to cry. It was better to push the feelings back. Keep them under a layer of stubbornness. And if you told yourself something hard enough a hundred times over and then a thousand more (*I'm fine I'm fine I'm fine I'm fine*), you started to believe it.

Now, tucked into the chair at the store, watching her

mother help a tourist decide between penguin and kitten salt shakers, she was glad she'd learned that early. The pain rose again, sinking into her skin like broken glass sank into her bike tires.

Caz.

Somewhere in the last three months, during the code-three runs to asthma attacks and code-two runs for pizza and ice cream, during his silences and his surprised barks of laughter, under his watchful eyes that warmed when he didn't know it, she'd been falling in love.

Love.

She'd honestly thought those afternoons when her stomach wouldn't settle, when her insides wouldn't stop flipping around like a dying fish, that she was becoming lactose intolerant. She gave up milk in her coffee, cheese for her burgers, and even went a whole week without ice cream.

Then she'd had him, and lost him, and only after he was gone did she realize what her sickness was.

Love.

What a stupid thing for a person, perfectly reasonable in every other way, to feel.

Her mother finished with the customer, and tottered back to her chair, *ploomp*-ing down and kicking off her heels. She patted her blond curls into place. Then she faced Bonnie, her eyes kind. For the first time, Bonnie could see Gramma Honor in her mother's gaze. When had her mother developed those lines across her forehead? When had she gotten those deep laugh lines at her mouth?

"Did you tell him how you feel?"

Bonnie felt color suffuse her face. *No.* No more crying. Her head hurt. No wonder she never cried. It was awful.

Her mouth was full of salt, and her eyes felt too puffy to fully close.

"I don't know how I feel."

"Oh, sugar. You don't?"

Love, love, love. The word reverberated in her mind, in her heart, in her very blood, it seemed.

If she could swallow her tears, she could push this down.

Couldn't she? "I can't tell him."

"You'll have to at some point."

"No." She shook her head, ignoring the pain in it. "I'll just fix it."

Her mother sighed. "Oh, my little fixer. You can't fix a broken heart like you can fix a broken bone."

"Sure I can." She could set it, keep it firmly in place, and let no one come near it for...for forever if that's the way it had to be.

Her mother's phone jingled with a text. She glanced at it. "Your father wants to know what he can do to help."

"You *told* him?"

Her mother looked guilty. "I'm worried about you."

Bonnie shook her head. It was bad enough her mother had seen her cry. If she accidentally teared up in front of her father, she'd probably have to kill herself with one of the penguin salt shakers from the front window. "No. He can't help."

Another cheery jingle from her mother's phone. Marge tilted her head. "Cheesy fries on bacon burgers for lunch? He'll bring them here."

Again, Bonnie shook her head, but her stomach grumbled, giving her away. "Oh, fine."

Her mother smiled and tapped a response.

Emotions. *Ugh.* Bonnie sure as heck didn't want this...

this incredible *weight* she felt inside her heart, as if it had been taken out of her chest, stomped on, and then chucked back inside, dirt and all.

Bonnie leaned her head back and closed her eyes. Then she wrapped her arms around her stomach. At least she felt hollow enough inside that she'd have some place to store this ridiculous pain.

CHAPTER 20

Table sixteen is complaining their soup is cold," Bonnie said frantically to Lexie. "What should I do? Nuke all their bowls? Eight of them will take forever, and then the first bowl will be cold again. Whose idea was it to do soup anyway?"

Lexie, cheerfully stirring a huge bowl of Caesar salad, said, "Tell them it's meant to be cold. It's French. *Vichyssoise.*"

"I thought it was tomato basil."

"Whatever. Make them buy it. Go. Shoo!"

The enormous apparatus bay at Station One had been cleared out, and all the rigs—the engine, the spare, the truck and the ambulance—were parked in the lot next door, ready to roll out if needed. Thirty tables stood under the soaring metal roof. Each table was covered with white tablecloths and fresh flowers from the farmer's market, bought that morning. The overhead lights, normally so glaringly bright, were turned off, and the whole room was glittering in candlelight. There had been a plan to have the bay doors open if it had been a warm night, but it was cold and rainy, so the doors were shut, the heaters were on, and the rain pounding down provided accompaniment to the laughter that filled the room.

It was, in a word, romantic.

Bonnie hated it.

Her eyes, horrible things that they were, couldn't stay off stupid Caz. He looked incredible, like a model posing for a firefighter calendar. All the guys wore their utility pants and house T-shirts with their station numbers on the back. On a lot of the older guys, the brown leather suspenders looked ridiculous as they bowed around the belly and crossed in back.

On Caz, though? Bonnie had almost tripped over her own boots when she'd seen him in the kitchen. He was freshly shaven, and he smelled great. He smelled *different*. Usually he smelled of soap and something more woodsy, like his shampoo was made of bark and rosemary. But tonight he smelled...expensive. Exactly the way he'd smelled the night he cooked for her at the ranch. As if he were on a date.

Which he decidedly was not. And certainly not with her.

He'd made it crystal clear that he had no interest in her. Whatsoever.

He hadn't called the next day. Or the next. When Bonnie had seen him at work two days later, his eyes had been clear, as if nothing had happened. "Hey, Bonnie," he'd said without meeting her eyes as they did the rig precheck. "How's it going?"

It was a question that didn't require an answer, though she'd stammered one anyway. "F-fine."

"Good, that's good. Do you know if they restocked the drugs last night?"

It was more than he usually said to her in the mornings.

But Bonnie wasn't glad he was talking. She was hurt and angry and sad and every time she figured out one emotion, she felt a new, different one, sweeping through her like the rain storms outside.

For two weeks, Bonnie had hidden everything by being uber-professional. Except for a kid call when they'd had to work hard together (the kid, who'd fallen off a three-story roof, had made it, thank God), they hadn't touched. They didn't bring up the night they'd spent together. They didn't talk about anything real, actually. Just the weather (fine, a little rainy), the workload (kind of busy, huh?), and who would drive (no, you go ahead). In the kitchen, Caz was quicker to laugh, and had even offered a couple of jokes of his own. The guys were starting to relax a bit around him.

That actually made her feel worse.

So tonight, she'd asked Lexie to assign her far away from whatever he ended up doing for the fundraiser, and with a sympathetic look, Lexie had agreed. "You still have to play Truth or Dare. That went out on all the fliers. It's Chief Barger with Tox, you with Caz."

"Fine," Bonnie had said. "I just don't want to serve drinks with him." Of course, that hadn't stopped her from trying to look as good as she could while still being in uniform. She wore a pair of utility pants she hadn't put on in a while because they'd always been a bit too small. She hadn't been eating with as much gusto as she usually did the last couple of weeks, and the pants fit her like a glove. Her T-shirt was brand new, dark blue, and fit her like second skin. Her suspenders bowed slightly to the sides of her B-cups, and she'd had Donna at the salon put bright highlights in her hair so her bob gleamed almost platinum. She'd done her makeup carefully, using a YouTube tutorial on "smoky eyes." To her astonishment, when she'd stepped back from the mirror, her eyes really *had* looked smudged, as if she'd put soot on her lashes, as if coal had streaked her eyes. As the standby medic at house fires, she'd seen her own face covered in fire soot plenty of times, and that had never been a good look for her. This, though... She looked like someone else. Someone prettier than she normally was.

Which was good. She'd seen it in Caz's eyes, over a table full of flowers and candles—he thought she looked good. She could tell it by the way he skated his eyes over her, down her body and back up again—greedily—as if he shouldn't be looking, as if he were stealing something from her that he shouldn't take.

And then he'd gone back to serving his table without smiling, without even waving a friendly hello.

Bonnie flew past hurt, confused, and sad, heading straight for mad. *Good. At least I'm working him out of my system.* She thumped another salad on Pastor Jacob's table and apologized when a tomato went flying.

The rest of the night flowed smoothly, thanks to Lexie and Coin's arrangements. Laughter tinkled from every table, and the wine (donated from Valentine's Forget-Me-Not winery, of course) flowed heavily. The serving firefighters didn't drink, of course (even though they were off-duty, they were still in uniform), but plenty of Bonnie's coworkers were in attendance as guests, dressed to the nines. The rest of the town was there, too, all of them in fancy finery—the mayor wore a peacock blue dress with sequins, and the city manager was in a tuxedo. The two richest couples in town—the ones who had built their enormous estates up in the hills—were there, the women wearing dresses that probably cost more than Bonnie's racing bike, and both the homeless Petes were in attendance, too, both of them with huge smiles and wearing rather grubby suits that didn't fit.

Lexie got on stage, still dressed in her *Fire Truck, Stay Back 100 Feet* apron. She led them through the courses of the meal, all locally sourced, and introduced the director of the Darling Bay Alzheimer's Support Initiative, who talked during the dinner itself. It was quiet while he spoke, only the clink of silverware floating above his words.

"*This* is the crisis we're not doing enough about. This is what many of us in this room face, with either ourselves or our loved ones destined to end in long-term dementia care. Every medic in this room knows what I'm talking about." David Green gripped the podium and leaned forward like a minister preaching to his flock. "They've been to the other care homes, the ones who lock their Alzheimer's patients in zones they can't break out of, and then just leave them to fade out, alone. Caring Village is a different model, and it's the only one we're backing, and we hope you will, too." He gestured to the PowerPoint displayed on the screen next to him. "You've seen the layout of the grounds. It will accommodate a hundred patients for the first year, which is only a small start, but at least it's a start. You see here, where this little grocery store is? It'll be stocked with fresh fruit and vegetables, and the cashier will be a nurse. Over here, at the post office, patients will be able to post and pick up mail if they want to, and we'll ferry it back and forth to the real post office in Darling Bay. The cafeteria is staffed by nurses dressed as food workers. See these four bus benches? They're one of the most popular things in the Swedish models we're copying—our patients will be able to wait for the bus which will be driven by another caretaker, ride around the 'town' a few times, and then get off where they like, still in Caring Village. They can ride all day if they want to, or they can sit on the bench and never get on."

Mr. Bartle had been one of Bonnie's favorite patients until he'd died the year before. A Houdini in striped pajamas, he could break out of his locked unit as easily as sneezing. Twice they'd been called by police in nearby towns when he'd been found, lost and wandering. The need for independent travel was one of Mr. Bartle's last desires to be forgotten, and if he'd been able to get on a bus safely and ride it for a while, things would have been so much simpler.

Bonnie wondered if Caz's father would like to ride a bus.

"The Village is set up to make a dementia patient feel independent as long as possible. For those who can no longer get around, there will be excellent standardized care, of course. But the Swedish research has shown us that Alzheimer's patients who stay active in their local community as long as possible stay healthier longer. While we're funded largely by grants at this point, we are a non-profit, and your contributions tonight make the difference in when we can open our doors."

Bonnie caught sight of Caz leaning against the metal cabinets near the bottle-filling room. His face was pale, and his eyes didn't leave the director's face.

She only realized she was staring when Lexie bonked her on the arm with a long set of tongs. "*Psst.* I need you."

Bonnie missed the next few things that happened on stage as she helped serve the flourless chocolate cake from Josie's Bakery. When she was done, though, the first round of Truth or Dare was soundly in session.

Tox sat on the left of the stage, looking like a huge, rigid block of muscle. Bonnie had watched him crash through fiery falling beams to rescue a litter of newborn kittens. The man had no fear. Normally. Right now, he looked terrified. On the other side of the small stage sat Chief Barger, looking much the same as always—in uniform, his handlebar mustache polished so that it almost shone, his face placid.

Lexie held up the cards collected from the audience. The stack of yellow cards were dares, the blue ones were truths. "Next one is a dare, gentlemen!" She shuffled the yellow cards and drew one with great ceremony.

"Okay. The dare is to put a full face of makeup on—eyes, lips, and cheeks." Lexie turned to face the crowd. "Folks, who's going to do this? Captain Tox Ellis, the tough guy who'd probably rather die than wear eyeliner, or Chief Barger, who at this very moment, is wondering how he'd go about getting lipstick out of his mustache?"

The bids came pouring in. Bonnie watched as hand after hand went up.

"A hundred on Tox! A hundred twenty-five on the Chief! Oh, that's more like it, two hundred on Tox, thanks, Gina! Now let's go higher."

The bidding ended at four hundred dollars for Tox. Grace Rowe got on stage and with great ceremony (and as if she'd planned for this to happen, Bonnie thought suspiciously), she made Tox up like a Vegas dancer: blue and green sparkly eye shadow, bright pink cheeks, red lips the color of blood. Tox was a good sport about it, adjusting the eyeliner so it was more pronounced, and grabbed Grace in a kiss afterward, leaving her lips stained and her eyes twinkling.

Two more rounds ensued, with the chief being bid upon to answer what thing he did regularly that he'd rather not admit (blushing, he said he picked his nose in the bathroom sometimes), and another dare went to Tox, who had to prank-call Caprese and ask if their refrigerator was running. When he said, "Then go out and catch it!" Lexie's microphone actually picked up the volume of Summer Darling's yelling, and the app bay filled with roars of laughter. Bonnie could picture Summer, surrounded by her three sisters in the kitchen, huffing and puffing about the prank, and it just made her laugh harder.

Bonnie looked around the large room—she could almost feel her heart get larger, more expansive. These were her people. Her family, both of blood and of choosing. Her father, over in the corner, had a hand on her mother's shoulder and she watched her mother smile at him. Her first-grade teacher, Mrs. Hawkins, much older but still dear to her, shot her a smile. Bonnie's heart lifted.

Then Lexie said, "Caz Lloyd and Bonnie Maddern to the stage, please! Ladies and gentlemen, you're in for a treat. Caz Lloyd is our quietest firefighter, and one of the newest members of our department. Let's drag him out of his shell. And you probably all know Bonnie, born and bred in Darling Bay, and you know she's scared of nothing. Except *maybe* of what's coming up next."

Bonnie looked at Caz, and even across the room, she could see the tightness at the corners of his eyes. Her heart dropped into her boots. This was going to be the worst thing ever.

CHAPTER 21

This was going to be the worst thing *ever*. Caz settled onto the hard plastic chair a few feet away from Bonnie on the small stage and gritted his teeth. Maybe if he concentrated hard enough, he could have one of those out-of-body experiences people were always talking about on late-night TV. He'd just float up and look down on what was happening on stage and when it was all over, he could rejoin himself and get himself the hell back to the ranch.

Bonnie, on the other hand, looked positively chipper. How did she do that? Did she actually *like* being up here, with all eyes on her? They deserved to be on her, that was true. She looked incredible, like all her features had been dipped into something iridescent. It wasn't makeup—he could tell that she had more on than usual (though she wore way less than the gobs piled on Tox's face right now). It was something else. An inner glow. She was heated inside—he could feel it from where he sat.

And blast it all, how he wished he could touch her skin to feel it himself. But he couldn't. He'd wrecked any chance of that when he'd kicked her out of his house. That had been his plan, after all—to damage that chance, to kill any glimmer of hope he could possibly have of having her, being near her.

How he was going to survive being in the rig with her, next to her, for months and months to come, he didn't know. He was going to lose his mind as well as most of his traitorous heart.

Transfer. He'd ask—no, beg—Chief Barger for a transfer.

On the floor below their seats on the stage, Lexie grinned. She was loving her role in this, obviously. If it hadn't been them up there, Caz could have taken pleasure in it, too. It was a fun thing to do, an amusing premise, unless you were the one on display next to the woman who heated you to diabolic temperatures without even trying.

Lexie held up a yellow card. "I'm going with a dare next. Let's see what we can get these two to do, shall we?" Slowly, *way* too slowly, she pulled out a card, and then she laughed. "Okay, whoever wrote this gets an official fire explorer sticker because this is awesome. The dare is: Spend the next round sitting on the other's person lap. Who's going to start the bidding?"

No way. It was a ridiculous, dumb, childish dare. Who would bid on it? But Caz was wrong. The bidding was fast and furious, and for a moment, it hung at five hundred dollars for Caz to sit on Bonnie's lap, which was entirely out of the question. Sure, Bonnie was strong, her arm muscles as defined as her bike-riding legs. But he'd crush her. The pause went on too long. Lexie was raising her hand to call it, when Caz heard a voice say, "Six hundred dollars to Bonnie."

It was his own voice doing the talking.

A delighted sound rose from the crowd, half laughter, half *ooohs*.

Lexie said, "Well! Didn't see that coming! Anyone want to bid against Caz Lloyd, who'd like to donate six hundred smackers to have Bonnie sit on his lap?"

An electric silence. Bonnie's lips twitched as if she might say something, but then she looked down at her hands.

"Going once, twice, sold to the man in the suspenders on the stage!"

Caz felt something lurch in his chest, something with hooves that was moving too fast. He was about to get run over by a stagecoach with short blond hair and the sweetest eyes in the west, and he wasn't sure he liked it.

But he sure wanted it.

CHAPTER 22

Bonnie could do this.

She could *totally* do this.

Looking out at the audience, she said, "Can someone get me a tequila shot? Maybe two?" Laughter rang. She looked down at her uniform. "Oh, wait. Crap, no alcohol for me. Fine, let's get this over with."

Over with. As if she'd ever wanted anything more than to sit in his lap. That was exactly the problem. Her whole body craved it, to the point of ridiculousness. She wanted to touch him even if they were in front of the whole dang town.

And that was dangerous.

Beyond dangerous. It felt suicidal.

But she stood. She faced the audience, her thumbs tucked under the front metal buckles of her suspenders. She gave them a cheeky snap and then sat on Caz's knee. The room showed its approval with another roar of laughter. Caz's face stayed deadpan, which made them laugh harder, but his expression wasn't quite still. Bonnie could feel the tension in his thigh muscles, an electric tautness that set her own nerves alight. And just there, at the corner of his mouth, she could see a small twitch, almost a tic.

So he wasn't in total control. Thank goodness it wasn't just her.

Lexie said, "All right, round two! This one is for the Truth. Here, Chief, now that you're off the stage, would you mind drawing a blue card for me?"

Chief Barger's mustache lifted in approval. He still looked a little pale, Bonnie noticed. The chief did well under pressure—no one better. But the political arena wasn't his favorite area, and he looked abjectly grateful not to be on the stage anymore. If Bonnie could pry her awareness away from how Caz's muscles felt under the backs of her legs, she would empathize with him.

Lexie took the card from the chief and laughed. "Oooh, this is a good one, too!"

Bonnie met Caz's eyes for the first time since they got on stage. Instead of finding the commiseration she'd been hoping she might find, she instead felt his hand go to the small of her back, where no one could see. His blue eyes darkened, and she couldn't read anything in their depths. She took a quick, indrawn breath at his touch and prayed she held it together.

Lexie said into the microphone, "The question is: What is the main thing that attracts you to the opposite sex? Do I hear a hundred for Bonnie to answer this one?"

The bidding flew upward—apparently the fact that she was sitting on Caz's lap was enough to titillate the easily-stirred (and rather liquored-up) crowd. Terry Dunlap, who owned the boat yard, finally yelled, "Five hundred, and they both have to answer!"

A satisfied silence followed, and heads nodded in the room.

Lexie said, "Sold to Terry! Who's first? Bonnie? Tell us truthfully, from your precarious position on that handsome firefighter's lap, what attracts you to a man?"

"His shoe size," said Bonnie as vampily as she could, dropping an eyelid in an exaggerated wink.

Over laugher, Lexie said, "Well, judging by the size of those shoes your feet are dangling above, you're doing just fine at this exact moment, ain'tcha? Moving on to Caz now. How about you? What draws you to the fairer sex?"

Caz didn't hesitate, and he didn't need the microphone for amplification. "Honesty."

The room's laughter fizzled. Caz's face was still, his voice cool. Bonnie wanted to stand, but the round wasn't over yet.

Lexie looked flummoxed. "Okay, well, I can bet you that's not what my boyfriend Coin would have said, but..."

"I thought this was Truth or Dare." Caz's voice projected to the back.

"It is."

"Then I want to hear the truth from Bonnie Maddern."

There wasn't a sound in the huge room, not even the rustle of a shoe on the concrete floor.

Bonnie's fingers flexed and she curled them tightly. "What are you doing?" she whispered.

"My shoe size isn't why you're attracted to me." His voice was still loud.

A delighted gasp rose in the audience and Bonnie could almost feel them leaning forward. She didn't dare look over where her mother and father were sitting. "Caz," she hissed.

"It's not a big deal. It's not like it's against policy, and neither of us are married. What made you kiss me in the first place?"

Another titillated buzz came from the audience.

"You kissed me first!" It wasn't true—another thing that wasn't true. That first kiss at Bud's Bar had been completely mutual—agreed to and acted upon together by both of them at the very same instant, she knew it.

Caz raised his eyebrows and stayed perfectly still, but he lowered his voice so that only she could hear him. "Okay, then. Why did you kiss me back?"

Bonnie's voice quieted, too. "I don't know." She wasn't sure if it was the truth, but she knew one thing—she didn't want to discuss it there in front of God and everyone.

His low voice teased, prodded. "Come on, Mad. 'Fess up. Why did you kiss me?"

"I'm not going to tell you."

"Fine," he said, leaning back, away from her, pointing at the crowd watching with greedy eyes. He raised his voice again. "Tell *them* why you kissed me."

Her mother sat openmouthed. Lexie covered her mouth with the rest of the stack of cards, her eyes dancing.

"You are *infuriating*," Bonnie said, steaming.

"*That's* why you kissed me?"

"And you're pompous and rude and you have no idea how to get along with anyone unless they're bleeding or seizing."

"So what you're saying is you're drawn to my bedside manner?" He nodded and smiled into the room. "I can see that."

More laughter. Caz had them in his pocket, and it was enraging. He went on, "As I remember it, we made out like teenagers after *you* touched my lips, wiping away mustard that wasn't actually there. You just said it was." He leaned back, putting a fraction of space between them, and looked her square in the eye.

Something icy slipped down Bonnie's spine, right

along the pathway that had just been so heated. She scrambled off his lap, almost tripping as she pushed away from him. He grabbed her arm to steady her and she hated that she had to touch him. When she was upright, she jerked herself away from him. No, *no,* the only answer to this kind of attack was to leave the stage, to stop talking to him entirely. Not only was he wrong, but he was completely out of line. "Can we finish this outside, please?"

He still looked easy in his skin, as if he didn't mind the stares. "I'm okay with hashing it out here."

"Well, I'm not." Bonnie stalked past the front tables, wading into the audience. The faster she got through the room, the faster she'd be able to suck in a breath, to grab the anger and hurt and force it into a shape she understood. The closest door was on the south wall, thankfully, so she didn't have to pass her mother's table. If she had, she probably would have just crawled under the tablecloth and clung to her mother's ankle like a three-year-old.

She heard Caz's footsteps following her. One of the homeless Pete's stage whispered, "I don't *get* it, man." Other than that, the room was perfectly silent.

The heavy metal door crashed open as Bonnie hit it with all her weight. Outside, the rain had slowed to a fine mist, and a thin moon struggled to shine through the eucalyptus trees.

"What the hell was that?" Bonnie felt attacked, and more than that, she felt humiliated. "You shouldn't have..."

"You lie in almost everything you do." Caz went on, his voice almost relaxed in its confidence. "You lie to your coworkers when you wake up, when you're that special kind of grumpy."

Bonnie was so angry her throat felt tight. She wasn't

sure she could manage to speak, but the words came out: "What are you *talking* about?"

"That's how you *start* your days. With untruth. You chirp your good mornings like a bluebird but all you want to do is stab the firefighter between you and the coffee pot. Your face is all wrinkled and your hair sticks straight up and you're trying to pretend your natural morning look is happy but it's not. You'd rather scowl till you've put away your second cup and nothing helps but that."

That was, infuriatingly, true. Just as she had when she was a child, Bonnie hated mornings with a purple passion but she faked her way through them at work. Lying in bed until ten and then taking a long bike ride was pretty much her idea of heaven on a day off. "But—"

"And when you have to drive the ambulance, instead of acting disappointed, which you are, you get all fake-chipper."

"I do not."

"You do." What *was* that lurking at the back of Caz's eyes? He continued, "You have this whole passive-aggressive cheerfulness thing that you drag over your head like you're hiding under a blanket. That whistle."

"What about it?"

Caz leaned against the wall of the building and pursed his lips, giving a low, slow whistle that echoed into the parking lot. "You whistle constantly. Like if you don't, you're going to say something you might regret."

Bonnie put her hands on her hips. Screw the fact that practically the whole town *and* her parents had watched their little exchange—she was too upset to care as much now as she knew she would later. "Anything else?"

"You lie to Valentine when you tell him you like his cooking."

Well, that was true. No one liked the nights when Valentine cooked, but they were on a rotation. And he was so inordinately proud of the food he made. If anyone else in the house had made crunchy rice, they would have laughed him right out of the station, but Valentine was so earnest about it, so excited every time he put the big spoons into his sweet-potato-oatmeal or gluten-free macaroni casserole, that Bonnie didn't have the heart to tell him that there was always a secret pizza delivery to the patio door every night he cooked.

"That's not fair. Who doesn't lie to him?" It was just a fact—a white lie was preferable to the truth sometimes. Why didn't Caz get that? He preferred to hurt people?

Bonnie turned her back on Caz and took a step away, toward where her bike was locked. She patted her pocket to make sure she had her house keys. It didn't matter that her raincoat was inside. She'd had enough humiliation for one night.

His voice followed her, strong and clear. "You lied at my house."

Her whole body stiffened.

"Bonnie." If a sound could physically wrap around her, his voice was the thing that could do it. She turned slowly. The rest of the world dropped away. There were just the two of them under the still-wet night sky. "At *my* house. You lied. Why?"

"About my virginity? I was teasing you, Caz."

"Not *that*. Do you really think I'm still mad about that? That was a stupid joke. It was nothing."

Confusion filled her body, her very bones. "Then..."

"You told my father he would be fine."

"Oh, Caz. I just—" She broke off. Her heart clattered as if she were in atrial fibrillation, rattling and thumping wildly in her chest. The thought raced through her mind that maybe that was where the technical shorthand had come from. Atrial fib. Afib. A fib. "It's just—"

"No *just*. If you'd only..." Caz paused and tugged on his ear so hard it looked like he wanted to pull it right off his head. "If you'd only been...*honest* with him. That would have been something. But you lied. To him."

Bonnie opened her mouth, but nothing came out.

"I can't forgive you for that."

The truth hit Bonnie with force. "That's not it."

"Excuse me?" Caz drew himself to his full height, and if she'd been a different woman, Bonnie might have felt cowed.

But she wasn't. She was the woman her grandmother had been proud of. "That's not what you're mad about. You *liked* that I said what I did to him. You liked that I made him feel better. I know you did." Bonnie was the woman her mother loved. She might not be good with emotion, and she was starting to admit perhaps that was something she should work on. (She'd cried on her mother's shoulder! Wasn't that enough of a start?) But she was great at her job-she knew that—and part of her job meant making people who felt terrible feel less scared. Sometimes that meant a half-truth.

And knowing what to say when didn't mean she didn't *know* the truth. Caz was upset she hadn't told him how she felt about him. That's what this was about.

She went on, "I know what you want me to say. You have that black-and-white way of looking at the world, and mine is messy, all purples and pinks and greens."

Caz's eyes were a lake of blue ice.

Bonnie went on. "There's a truth to everything, and then there are shades. Your father will be fine because that's the truth. If he dies right this moment, while we're here, he'll be fine. I believe that. Besides." She dug her fingers into her palms and said the next words slowly. "I didn't tell him he was going to be okay for his sake. I said that for you. Half the things we say at deathbeds are for the living, not the dying."

"He's not—" The sound was ripped from Caz's throat, low and painful.

"He is. You know he is. If you don't admit that, then *you're* the one lying." Bonnie knew she'd crossed a line, but it was too late to mark boundaries. "He won't make it much longer."

"He's strong. He's—"

Bonnie put her hand to her stomach, almost able to feel the knots beneath her fingers. "If you believe that, then you'd think it was just fine I told him he was going to be okay. He *was* strong. He's not now. Now is the time you have to give your strength to him."

Caz's face went dark. "You're out of line."

"Me? You left your cabin, your old job, everything you cared about to take care of him, but you've done it with resentment and bitterness at leaving your old life behind. You think that's really what he would have wanted? You think he *appreciates* that? Your job is to filter the world around him. To make him feel cared for. And you're failing at it."

"He has no idea what's going on around him."

"But *you* do." Bonnie didn't know where she found the air to say the next words. "Take care of your father, Caz. Show him you care, that you believe in his strength. That's the only truth that matters."

It wasn't, not to her. The truth that mattered to *her* was that her heart was breaking, but she could deal with that later, alone, in her bed, under the covers. She'd stay there for the next ten years or so. She might even cry. The whole time.

Caz's face was bleak, as if she'd taken away something he'd worked his whole life for.

Bonnie stayed still. She had no courage left.

Caz said, "Truth or Dare, right?"

She nodded.

"Truth, then," said Caz. "Are you in love with me, Maddern?"

The only answer was *yes*. It sang in her veins. *Yes, yes, yes.*

But she said, "I don't know." She stood in front of him as the mist turned back into a fine drizzle, her uniform doing nothing to protect her from the naked feeling of her skin beneath the fabric. "Are *you* in love with *me?*"

He looked right into her eyes. "No," he said.

Caz went back in the door, into the app bay, leaving her alone in the dim moonlight, dashing away the unforgivable tears from her cheeks.

CHAPTER 23

It was a lie.

It was the worst lie of all.

That said, he wouldn't—couldn't—take it back. She'd said she didn't know how she felt about him. So him saying he didn't love her...well, maybe if he worked really hard at it, if he made it a full-time job, someday he could make it true.

"Come on, Dad." Caz carefully propped his father up on the pillows. "Can you stay put just for a little while? Just settle in. That's right. Just like that." He'd sent Joyce to bed —she'd looked exhausted when he'd gotten back to the ranch.

"You sure?" she'd asked. Her face had been pale. "It's a bad night."

"I'm sure. I'll stay with him."

"Caswell, we need to talk about—"

"No, thank you," he'd said. As if he were declining dessert. No, thank you, he would not talk about moving his father to a facility where they'd stick him in a bed and strap him down until he died, alone, unknown and unloved. No, thanks. Not today. Or ever.

"But—"

"Good night, Joyce." Caz had kissed her on the cheek, surprising himself. "Thank you for being here."

"Of course." She'd gone pink and smiled. "Of course."

Now, hours later, Tony Lloyd was only beginning to settle down. For the first time all night, he seemed to listen when Caz soothed him.

"That's it, Dad. Just close your eyes."

Tony's eyes closed. "Story."

Caz jumped. "What?"

Tony pressed his lips together in a tight line.

"Dad?"

His father stayed silent.

Had he really asked for a story? Or was that just another noise his father made, words that weren't really words, sound that carried no meaning?

Caz picked up the wolf he'd been carving for weeks now. It still wasn't done. Something about the legs, maybe, or the muzzle? Something was wrong, and he couldn't tell what it was.

"Story." Tony's eyes were open, and he met Caz's gaze almost as if he were still himself. As if Dad were still in there. Somewhere.

Bonnie's voice came back to Caz. *To make him feel cared for.*

"What kind of story?"

Silence.

Of course his father was silent. What was Caz thinking? That his father knew what he was asking for? Stupid. So stupid to think that.

But if he did...

"Okay," started Caz. "I'll tell you about..." *Bonnie*. He only wanted to talk about Bonnie. About the way her hair lit in sunlight, and about how her lips looked when she pursed them in a whistle. About how he'd screwed up maybe bigger than he had in his whole life.

He'd lied to her.

Tony's hands moved fitfully, pulling at the blanket that covered him. Caz smoothed it.

The one thing he'd wanted from Bonnie, she couldn't give him. But instead of giving her the truth, *I'm so in love with you it hurts, so in love with you I'm blind to anything else*, he'd lied for the first time in memory. It was a flat-out, bald-faced ugly-as-sin lie. The worst untruth.

He still didn't know why he'd done it.

"Story," said Tony again. "Cabin."

"Dad?" Caz wanted to lunge at the idea. Anything to take his mind off *her*.

"Cabin."

Maybe his father *was* in there. "Okay. Great." Caz pulled his straight-backed chair—the one his father had helped him make so many years before—closer to the bed. "So. The cabin is almost done. You were right about the flooring, by the way. I ran the first boards perpendicular to the joists, just like you said." His father had talked about how to put in a floor years before Caz had started building the cabin, but he'd never forgotten what he'd said. While he'd worked on the walls and setting the chimney stones and buying the glass for the windows, he'd remembered his father's words on construction, pretending his father was there to help.

That, in itself, was kind of a lie, wasn't it?

But Tony's eyes were still on him. They still had this moment. Together.

"Anyway. I still have to put the final touches on it. I have no furniture. Every room is still empty. I kind of like it that way, I gotta admit. Remember what you said about every room's echo being different? I love that I know how my footsteps sound in the kitchen versus the bedroom. When I buy the furniture, I want to know that..."

What? What did he want to know? Why did knowing Bonnie's favorite color seem so important to him suddenly?

"You'll take..." His father's words trailed off. "Take..."

Caz leaned forward, wanting to grab each sound his father made. "Take what? Take you?" He couldn't. His father couldn't make the trip, unless he was sedated the whole time, and even then his breathing would make it too difficult...

But Caz took a deep breath. "Of course, Dad. I'll take you." Once he said it, he was astonished at how good it felt.

He believed it, too. That was the strangest part.

"I'll put you in the truck, and we'll go up the coast road. Then we'll cut inland through the redwoods—they're still your favorite tree, I bet. Mine, too. We'll get there before dark and even though I have no furniture, I still have that little hibachi. I set it out on the deck, and I have a bag of charcoal, ready to go. I haven't cooked a steak there yet, but we'll do that together."

Tony gave a sigh and closed his eyes. Was it a happy sigh? An uncomfortable one?

Caz kept talking. Kept hoping. "So we'll sit out on the porch, and then you'll get to see how the light drops there over the pond to the west. It's why I put the front porch where I did. Every night, to be able to sit there and rest, and watch the way the water ripples as the trout grab the early evening moths... You'll love it. We'll go." He said it again. "We'll go soon."

"Her."

Caz held his breath.

"Not me. Her," said his father, his eyes still closed.

Tony hadn't made this much sense in six months. Maybe more.

How could Caz trust the words? How could he trust they weren't just nonsense? The garbled brain of his father whirring in a body that was shutting down?

Then it sunk into him, into his very bones.

Caz got to choose what he believed. The truth was... his own.

He got to make it. To believe it.

He felt rocked back, a sonic boom sounding in his chest.

He got to choose the truth.

"I'll take her. To the cabin. I will. If she'll have me, that is."

His father opened his eyes once, looked right at him, and then closed them again. In that glance was everything Caz needed to know. What he needed to believe.

"I can't promise anything. I lied to her, and I'm not sure she's going to forgive me, Dad. But I'll try." He looked at the wooden wolf, still clutched in his hand. He knew what was wrong with it now.

He didn't want to be the lone wolf. Not anymore.

Caz wanted to be with Bonnie. He wanted to love her as long as the sun burned overhead, and when it collapsed, he wanted to love her through the black eternal night.

"I promise you this, Dad. I'll try my damnedest."

CHAPTER 24

Lexie was in the parking lot fighting with her car when Bonnie rode up on her bicycle. Lexie was cursing, pulling at a bag that appeared to be wedged in the backseat.

"You code four?"

Lexie scowled at Bonnie's backpack. "I have too much *stuff.* I don't know how you bring so little to work. How do you *do* that?"

It was a relief, seeing Lexie first. Bonnie was terrified of coming to work, of the moment she'd have to face Caz, scared to death she wouldn't be able to pull it off when she was near him. She wasn't even sure *what* she had to pull off (breathing? Being alive? Pretending she wasn't totally, life-alteringly and tongue-numbingly in love with him?) but she was going to have to work hard at it. So hard.

Bonnie could hide the truth when she had to, yes. She could keep her emotions in check and not show when a bad call got to her. When her aunt had died of a heart attack the year before, Bonnie hadn't cried once—once again, she'd stayed solid for her mother to lean on. Someone had to pick up the pieces.

But hiding how she felt about Caz...

Well, she would just *have* to. It wasn't like she had much of a choice.

"I have stuff." Bonnie hiked her backpack higher onto her shoulder. "Granola bars. Hard-boiled eggs in case the food fund runs out again. My uniform shirts that I didn't iron. Hey, why are the rigs all parked in the south lot?"

"You have all that in that little backpack?" Lexie pushed her hair out of her red face and pulled harder on the straps of her bag.

"Let me help." Bonnie leaned her bike against Valentine's truck, and both she and Lexie pulled. The bag finally came free, spilling produce all over the ground. Carrots, spinach, peas, blueberries—all of it went bouncing on the concrete, looking like an overturned farmer's market table.

"Crap," sighed Lexie. "That's like thirty bucks right there."

"What are you doing with all this?" Bonnie picked up a beet and held it up by its green end. "Where's your chocolate stash?"

Lexie sighed. "Juicing. Smoothie-ing. Something. It's Coin's idea..." Her hand went to her lower abdomen.

Bonnie gasped. "You're pregnant."

Lexie blushed. "Nah..."

"You *are*. I can tell. Look at you. Oh, Lexie!"

Lexie's face was a mixture of relief and dismay, a smile followed by a grimace. "You can tell? I haven't even put on a pound yet. I've lost two, in fact, with all this stupid health food stuff. Don't tell anyone. It's still a secret for now, just until I get big as a house...and..."

"Lexie!" A handful off spinach in one hand, a bunch of cilantro in the other, Bonnie hugged her. "I'm so happy for you."

"Yeah, well. Thanks." A huge grin. "We're happy."

"Good."

Lexie shoved three bananas in her canvas bag and went for two apples that were making a break for it. Then she held up a carrot. "You think this is clean? It only hit the ground for a second, right? And what about you?"

"Me?" Bonnie made her voice bright. "What about me? This is about you!"

"You took last tour off."

"What are vacation hours for, huh? Just stacking 'em up, doing nothing with them...All work and no play, you know."

Lexie looked at her suspiciously and took a bite of carrot. Around the mouthful, she said, "Ten days off in a row isn't like you. You go anywhere?"

Bonnie thought of how she'd gone between the couch and the bed. Several times, in fact. "Nowhere special. Saw a few people." On her TV.

"How are you and..." Lexie's voice trailed off.

"Caz?" Bonnie folded her lips and thought about the question. How were they? They were done. That was the simple answer.

The more difficult answer was something she'd spent long dreary hours on the couch thinking about while the television flickered reality shows at her. She'd been right about sticking to her guns when she told Caz he had to shelter his father, that he had to make this world—the current one—the most pleasant place possible for a strong cowboy who was dying ignominiously.

But Caz was right, too. She'd hidden her real feelings for him behind her anger and confusion.

He didn't feel the same way she did. He'd told her so. Oh, he felt something for her, sure. She knew that. He felt lust, and he felt excitement. He'd been clear, though, that he didn't feel anything more than that.

Bonnie was just going to have to handle that.

She had no idea *how*. But she would handle it, just like she always handled the difficult things.

And she would only cry at home, alone.

Lexie was still staring at her, apparently waiting for the answer.

"Um, we're..."

"Whoops. See you!" Lexie waved the carrot and four bags in Bonnie's direction and hurried toward the building.

From behind her, Bonnie heard the sound of a bicycle bell.

"Hiya." Caz coasted to a stop, dismounting from the bike. Instead of looking like a kid, he looked like a cowboy stepping off a horse, fluid and easy. He made the bike seem like a tool, something he *used*. He made it sexy. Damn him.

"Hi," Bonnie said. She was grateful her voice worked. "You look...natural on that."

"What do they say? It's like riding a bike?" He smiled.

How was she possibly going to live through this? A whole forty-eight hours of him? Looking like that? His jaw was broad and clean-shaven, as if he'd just wiped off the shaving cream, and his eyes were clear.

Nerves shot along her spine. "Why are you on your bike?"

"Why are you on yours?" he countered.

"Because...I love it."

"Ah. Me, too."

"You love your bike."

"I do. I love lots of things I'm not very good at admitting to."

The nerves turned to lightning. Bonnie wouldn't... couldn't... She changed the subject. "You rode from the ranch?"

"Yep."

"All the way? That's a long ride."

"Worth it," was all he said, and he looked at her.

Bonnie felt a warmth start, just under her skin.

Caz leaned his bike up against the rack and locked it as if it were something he did every day. Then he straightened, and reached for her handlebars. She let him take her bike without protesting. If stars fell to the ground and lay there sparkling, she would have been less surprised.

"I missed you last week," Caz said.

"You missed me." Was this all she was going to do? Just restate his words, inanely, over and over?

"I did."

"You..." She felt anger then, bright as sparks from a bonfire leaping in the starless sky. "You can't just...*say* that."

"I'm pretty used to saying what I want to say."

"I know," Bonnie said. "It's not your most attractive feature."

Undaunted, Caz said, "What would you say is?"

"Your ability to be quiet for a whole forty-eight hours." It was snippy and Bonnie wanted to take it back as soon as she said it.

But Caz said, "Fair enough." He rocked back on his heels as if he had all day to look at her.

For a moment, Bonnie wished he did. The way he was drinking her in with his eyes, the way he looked at her like she was something beautiful, something special and good...

"We'd better get in there," she said, pointing at the door.

"Guess so," said Caz, as if he were in no hurry at all to

get changed into his uniform. As if he all he wanted to do was stand in the sunshine with her.

Bonnie ached. "I have to get dressed," she said.

"Okay. Then meet me at the rig, will you? I have something for you."

CHAPTER 25

Bonnie took her time putting on her work clothes. She took another shower, even though she'd taken one at home before she left the house. She stood with her chin on the windowsill and watched the trees swaying behind the station as the hot water beat down on her. Closing her eyes, she allowed herself to imagine, just for a moment, the way Caz had touched her that night—the one night they'd had together.

It would be enough.

It would *have* to be enough.

The overhead pager came to life with a squawk. "Maddern, to the app bay. Maddern, app bay." Tox's voice. She peered suspiciously out the window to see if anyone was lurking in the flowerbed again, but she saw nothing.

She toweled off quickly and put her uniform on. At least if Tox wanted her in the bay, it wouldn't be just her and Caz out there—alone—with the ambulance.

When Bonnie pushed open the heavy door that led to the bay, she blinked. Then she blinked again, harder.

It was dark inside, but that was nothing new. The only

windows in the huge room were the small glass panes in the roll-up doors, and they never let in much light.

What stopped her in her tracks were the candles.

They burned in two rows on the floor, making a well-defined path to the stage.

The stage! It was still set up.

Rather, it must have been re-set-up, because it had to have been taken apart in the ten days she'd had off work. But this explained why she'd seen the rigs parked outside—there was nothing between Bonnie and Caz but forty paces and daytime candlelight.

And Caz was wearing a tux.

The tips of her fingers tingled and her mouth went dry. If Bonnie had thought he looked devastating in his utilities, he looked twice as dangerous in the dark black fabric, the jacket sitting perfectly on his wide shoulders, a nervous smile hovering over his bow tie.

"What are you doing?" But Bonnie's voice was soft, and they were still miles apart.

Caz just stood there. As if he was waiting for *her*.

She took a few steps forward, tentatively. Then she looked over her shoulder. Were the guys going to jump out at her? Was this some kind of grotesque practical joke? It was Tox, after all, who'd made the announcement over the speaker that got her to the bay. What if this was somehow making fun of her for how she'd come across at the fundraiser? Or if they were all teasing her for sleeping with him? Would they do that? They were her work brothers. They shouldn't...

But Caz's fingers twitched at his sides, and she could see the tension in his jaw, even across the wide room. He was as shaken as she was by the thing that pulled between them.

She took three more steps toward him. Slowly. Then five. Finally, she was close enough for him to hear her.

"You're not in uniform," she said.

He looked down at his tux. "Nope."

"What if we get a medical?"

"Well, now." There was a country cowboy twang in his voice to match the black cowboy boots on his feet. "I guess you'll have to drive while I strip-change in the back of the ambo."

A vivid picture of what he looked like underneath the tux played behind her eyes, and she felt her cheeks heat. "What are you doing?"

"Apologizing."

"For what?" She was the one, after all, who'd told him callously his father was dying. She was the one who had lied to him, saying she didn't know if she was in love with him or not. Chicken. That's all she was. "Caz, I have to tell you something."

"No, wait." He reached down for her hand and pulled her up on stage with him. "Let me do this."

Bonnie gave a high-pitched giggle that was nothing more than frantic nerves. She looked around again. "Are we being recorded or something?"

Caz shook his head. "No."

Good lord. She felt even more ridiculous. "I know. I know you're not. I don't know what I'm saying..." Just being this near him put her brain on the fritz. Soon she'd fizzle and melt into the ground, and they'd have to scrape her off the concrete like old gum.

"Bonnie. Listen." He took her other hand. "Listen to me, okay? I'm—"

The tones pealed through the station as the lights flashed and the doors rolled up. Lexie's voice rolled out through the station speakers, "Engine One, Rescue One, medical, female down."

"*Crap*." Caz gripped her hands tightly for one more second, then let go. "I guess I'm getting naked in the ambulance."

CHAPTER 26

I n the fire service, there was driving code three—going as fast as you could possibly go—and then there was the unofficial code-three-and-a-half, which was driving just a little bit faster than that. When Lexie gave the update, saying an elderly female had been found down in her house, alone and bleeding, Bonnie stepped it up to the latter.

"It's Ava!" she yelled over her shoulder. Behind her, Caz was sitting on the gurney and had his tux trousers off, but it looked as if he'd forgotten to take off his cowboy boots first.

"Who?" He yanked harder on the pants.

Bonnie tried desperately not to ogle his red briefs. "You know, I broke her toilet!"

"She's never really hurt," said Caz, tugging at his left boot. "She probably needs her coffee pot cleaned or something. You should slow down if you want me to be decent by the time we get there..." But his voice was worried, too. The call hadn't come in from a medical alarm—according to dispatch, it had come from a neighbor.

The house, in disrepair last time, looked even worse on

the inside this time. There were dishes piled in the sink that might have been there for weeks, and Ava, lying on the floor of the washroom just off the kitchen, looked so thin Bonnie's heart hurt.

"Oh, dear," Ava said, grasping for glasses she wasn't wearing. "They sent me the handsome one again, didn't they? And me without my lips on."

Caz smiled and kneeled next to her. "You've got quite a bump on your noggin there, don't you?"

Bonnie reached for the gauze and butterfly strips. They'd clean out the head wound, but she was going to need stitches at the hospital. "Do you know when you fell, Mrs. Simon?" The bleeding was barely a trickle—it had to have been hours before.

Ava Simon blinked at her. "Who's Mrs. Simon?"

Bonnie felt even more concern. "I'm sorry, I—"

The older woman laughed. "I'm just teasing. I have all my faculties, more's the pity, or I could have had a lot more fun hallucinating down here for hours. I fell last night, when I was getting supper ready."

Bonnie glanced at the counter behind her and saw the can of black beans, halfway opened, the can opener next to it.

"I like beans," said Ava with a little flip of her hand. "You'd be surprised at how little you can get by on when you're my age. I made a single bag of walnuts last three months."

Bonnie gasped.

Ava laughed. "Got you again!" But then she grimaced, her laugh collapsing, as Caz touched her side. "Ooof. It's bad, huh?"

Her left hip was broken, Bonnie could tell by the way she was folded up on herself.

It was only going to get worse for Ava Simon. How many times had Bonnie seen exactly this? An elderly person in good health, taken down by a hip, and never released from the hospital again. Ava was already frail. She wouldn't stand a chance.

Caz said to Ava, "You're going to be fine."

Bonnie stared at him.

Ava's eyes brightened. "You think so?"

"I know so. You're going to be just fine."

Ava looked at Bonnie, searching her face. "You think I can trust this young man?"

Caz followed Ava's gaze. Both of them waited for Bonnie's answer.

"Yes," Bonnie said. "I think you can."

CHAPTER 27

At the hospital, after making sure Ava Simon was tucked in and full of meds that made her flirt woozily with every orderly that wandered by, Bonnie and Caz stood in the hallway leaning on the same wall.

They were inches away from each other. Around them, nurses bustled, family members hurried, doctors ambled. But to Bonnie, there was no one else in the hall. He was so close to her she could feel the heat from his shoulder, smell the scent of wood shavings and soap.

Her pinky finger touched his, and it felt like a burn. Or a kiss.

She didn't move her hand away.

He didn't, either.

"Did you mean that?" Caz asked, his voice as soft as it had been when they'd been in bed together, as soft as it had been that night when he'd told her how she felt in his arms. "What you said back there about trusting me?"

Bonnie paused before answering. Her heart did that weird fluttery thing again. "If I say yes, will you tell me what you were doing in the app bay? On the stage, in your tux?"

"I was just hoping."

Her breath hitched in her chest. "For what?"

"For you to forgive me for what I said."

"What you said to me was crap."

"I know. And I'm sorry." He cleared his throat. "I'm so sorry."

Bonnie counted the beeps of a heart monitor she could hear in the next room. When she got to thirty, she said, "But what I said about your dad... and what I couldn't tell you...I should have—"

"No, you shouldn't have," he said, turning to face her. His crystalline-blue eyes warmed. "I was the one who made all the mistakes. I was furious with you, with what you could do to me without even trying. You made my dad feel better, and that's like winning the lottery for him. And me. That same night, you made me feel like I could touch the sky. Then, I not only shut you out, but I kept you out, and then I told you we had nothing together." He paused, and touched her cheek so lightly she wondered if she imagined it. "I couldn't have been more wrong. *That's* what I was doing on the stage. I was trying to change the outcome, to make it right."

Something joyful tugged inside her. "So..."

"So. I'm asking if we can move forward."

Yes. Bonnie's heart said yes. Her brain stalled, though, and her mouth said, "Where?"

"Wherever you are. I don't care where that is. That's where I want to be."

"Huh." It seemed as if she'd lost all the other words she'd ever known. She wanted to—longed to—lean forward and wrap her fingers around the collar of his work shirt, but she stayed still. "Huh."

"I know you can't tell me how you feel."

Bonnie opened and shut her mouth. She *wanted* to.

Caz reached forward and tugged on the pocket of her sweatshirt. She swayed toward him. "I can say it for both of us. I love you."

The words he said were huge and yellow—enormous balloons of delight that soared away, taking the stopper in her throat with it. "I love you, too," said Bonnie.

Caz looked both shocked and delighted, as if someone had just handed him the thing he wanted the most, the thing he thought he'd never find. "You what?"

Bonnie laughed. "I love you." The words tasted of salt. Nothing about them felt normal, but they felt right. Her truth. Her whole truth. "I'm in love with you, Caswell Lloyd."

"Holy—" He broke off and gave a ranch-hand whoop. "You're telling me how you feel." It wasn't a question.

"No," she realized. "I'm telling you what I know." That was the difference. Feelings changed, emotions swayed. That was why they couldn't be trusted, couldn't be believed.

Knowing was something else.

Bonnie knew her parents loved her, and she knew she loved them back. She knew Darling Bay was where she was meant to be, she knew she had the best job in the world, and she knew it just as surely as she knew how to whistle.

Most of all, though, she knew she loved the man in front of her, the one whose eyes said he knew it, too.

"One question. No, wait. Two."

Caz grinned. "As many as you want."

"Kiss me?"

He did, thoroughly. And she kissed him back. His lips were as hot as his fingertips were cool, and if they hadn't been standing in the middle of the emergency room hallway, Bonnie might have gone looking for the briefs she'd seen in the rig. A nurse yelled, "Get a room!"

Bonnie pulled back, but stayed firmly where she was, in his arms. "That wasn't the first question. The first one is will you take me to your cabin?"

"It's pretty empty. Only if you help me fill it with things we love."

She lost her breath as happiness filled her like helium. She took a few seconds to find it again and then asked, "Will you carve me a bicycle someday?"

Caz laughed.

Then he pulled a tiny block of wood from his pocket and showed her the minuscule pedals.

DID **you enjoy this book by Rachael Herron?**

JOIN RACHAEL'S list

Stay up-to-date on new releases
and *automatically* be entered for giveaways!
(Psst - get a free full-length romance (*Cora's Heart*) just for joining.)

CHAT WITH RACHAEL:
Facebook
Twitter
Blog

Patreon

ABOUT RACHAEL HERRON

RACHAEL HERRON IS the bestselling author of the novels *The Ones Who Matter Most, Splinters of Light* and *Pack Up the Moon* (all from Penguin), the five-book Cypress Hollow series, and the memoir, *A Life in Stitches*. She received her MFA in writing from Mills College, Oakland. She teaches writing extension workshops at both UC Berkeley and Stanford and is a New Zealand citizen as well as an American. You can find her at RachaelHerron.com.

ARE YOU CREATIVELY STUCK?

ARE you trying to live creatively but reach for the remote instead of doing what you're *really* drawn to, the thing you feel meant to do? For as little as a buck a pop, you can get Rachael's essays on living your best creative life. Come watch the video and learn more: Patreon.

KEEP READING **FOR A SNEAK PEEK OF THE NEXT BOOK!**

DON'T MISS a minute in Darling Bay! **One unforgettable town, three standalone series**

(read them in any order!). So many ways to fall in love!

THE FIREFIGHTERS OF DARLING BAY:
Playing with fire has never been this fun...

BLAZE: Tox and Grace - Book 1
Burn: Coin and Lexie - Book 2
Flame: Hank and Samantha - Book 3
Heat: Caz and Bonnie - Book 4
Or get all four together on sale, HALF OFF! Save $5.97!
The Firefighters, Boxed Set

THE SONGBIRDS OF DARLING BAY:
Nashville meets the Gilmore Girls in this heartwarming new trilogy of estranged country-singing sisters seeking true love (and their way back to each other).

THE DARLING SONGBIRDS, Book 1, March 2016
The Songbird's Call, Book 2, September 2016
The Songbird's Home, Book 3, March 2017

THE BALLARD BROTHERS **OF DARLING BAY:**
The Bachelor meets The Property Brothers: Love, property, and construction. What could possibly go wrong?

. . .

ON THE MARKET, Book 1, June 2016
  Build it Strong, Book 2, October 2016
  Rock the Boat, Book 3, January 2017

STANDALONE NOVELS:
Women and families finding their ways back to what really matters: each other:

THE ONES Who Matter Most
  Splinters of Light
  Pack Up the Moon

CYPRESS HOLLOW ROMANCES 1-5:
Knit-lit with more heat than just wool could ever provide:

HOW TO KNIT a Love Song
  How to Knit a Heart Back Home
  Wishes & Stitches
  Cora's Heart
  Fiona's Flame
  Eliza's Home (Historical Novella)

MEMOIR:
Rachael's life as seen through the sweaters she's knitted:
  A Life in Stitches

. . .

KEEP READING **for a Sneak Peek**

of the first book in *The Songbirds of Darling Bay* series, a full-length, heartwarming new romance from Rachael Herron!

EXCERPT OF THE DARLING SONGBIRDS:

CHAPTER 28

The saloon had always looked old-fashioned, but now it resembled a set in a ghost town. The boards creaked under Adele Darling's feet as if they hadn't been stepped on since women wore hoop skirts. Cobwebs on the porch slung themselves from top beams to bottom ones, and an old wagon wheel leaned against a hitching post in front. It was as if the sidewalk had been poured right around the post, and her Toyota hybrid looked completely wrong parked next to it. It should have been a horse.

The problem was that Adele wasn't in an old western, or a ghost town. Darling Bay was the sleepy gold-rush town her great-grandfather had given his name to.

The town she'd left for good a long time ago.

There was a hand-drawn sign that said: *Hours – 11 AM–2 AM*. She glanced at her cell phone. Almost noon, and the doors were locked. Awesome.

She knocked on the wood next to the iron screen door.

"That won't do you no good."

Adele spun. "Sorry?"

The exceedingly short woman standing on the step

below her wore a long, oversized blue dress that hung on her like a sack. Somewhere in her mid-sixties, she had a well-creased face, like a crumpled envelope. A dozen or more necklaces dangled around her neck, crystals and quartz and what looked like actual feathers, on tarnished silver chains. Her short grey hair stuck up in spikes as if she'd just run her hands over it roughly, but her smile was wide. "He ain't here yet."

Adele wasn't sure who *he* was. "Okay . . ."

"But if you reach up above the door," the woman pointed, "yeah, right there. You're a tall one, ain't you? Grab that key for us, will you?"

It wasn't that Adele was tall at five foot five. It was more like the woman was eye level to her elbow. "Got it." Now that the key was in her hand, Adele had no idea what to do with it. It wasn't like she would just unlock the bar's front door. Would she?

She didn't have to make the decision. In a move so quick it surprised her, the woman snatched the key from her palm and unlocked the iron security door, swinging it wide open and barreling through the wooden half-door as if she owned the place, which Adele knew for a fact she didn't.

"Sometimes I gotta open up for him, you know?" The woman moved to the right and snapped on two light switches, and then headed for the bar. She was a low, fast-moving bowling ball in blue. "It's usually harder 'cause it's tough for me to reach that key. It's not like I mess with the till or nothin', I just help him out where I can."

Adele trailed behind the woman. This wasn't the situation she had imagined herself in when she'd awoken this morning. All she'd known four hours ago in her San Francisco hotel was that she had a long drive up the coast. When she got to Darling Bay, she figured she would plan her next move.

So she'd gotten in her rental car and headed north. Highway One wound through the redwoods, darting out to the rocky coast and back inland again. She'd stopped once to stretch her legs, and had stood cliff-side watching elephant seals slap themselves up and down the coarse sand. It took a bit more than three hours to get to Darling Bay, a long-enough drive to make her feel as far from Nashville as she'd ever felt.

She used to be used to this feeling. This used to be home.

And now she had exactly no idea what that meant.

"You want a drink, dearie?"

Adele blinked. "I'm sorry . . . Who are you?"

"Well, I suppose I could ask you the same thing."

That was fair. "I'm Adele Darling."

"Oh, my *God*. You *are*."

Crap. Adele should have just said her first name. What was she thinking? Nowhere else would her last name have raised more than a vaguely puzzled eyebrow. *Sounds familiar . . . can't place it.* But not here.

The woman clutched at her pile of necklaces. "They didn't tell me that."

"Who?" Adele was feeling more confused by the second. "I don't think anyone knew I was coming."

"But they usually tell me everything." She held up a chain that had a pink piece of stone at the end and peered at it closely.

"Your necklaces tell you these things?" Adele kept her voice soft. Maybe it was better not to startle her.

The woman stared at Adele as if she were crazy. "Not my necklaces. My *dreams*."

"Ah."

"Of course, it's not like they're always right. Sometimes they tell me a storm is coming when all that's going to happen is I forget to take the kettle off the stove. Same thing." She waved her arms above her head. "Clouds of steam. Just in my kitchen. You see?"

Adele nodded carefully.

"Where are the other two?" The woman peered behind Adele as if she were somehow hiding her sisters.

"Not with me." Nothing could be truer. "I didn't get your name." Adele held out her hand.

The woman's shake was firm. "Norma."

"And you're the bartender?"

Norma laughed heartily, but she spread her palms on the top of the bar as if to negate her next statement. "Oh no, not me. You're a funny one. I'm just a drinker, from a long line of the same. Speaking of which, what can I make you?"

Not the bartender, then, but not *not* the bartender. "How about a Coke?"

"With rum? And can I read your tarot cards?" Norma asked hopefully.

"I'm good on both, thanks." It was a bit early to start pounding liquor. "So if you're not the bartender, and the saloon was supposed to open at eleven . . ."

"Oh, he'll be here."

"Who will?" This was beginning to feel like a game of Who's On First.

"Nate."

"Nate?"

"You don't know him?"

"I haven't been here in a while," Adele said. If a while meant eleven years. She'd been far away from Darling Bay, sometimes as far as a person could get. "*When* do you think he'll be here?"

Norma frowned and held one of her necklaces, looking upward as if the answer hung in the cobwebbed rafters. "Soon." Then she filled a glass with Coke and slid it towards Adele. "Here you go. Now, tell me everything. How're your sisters? You know, my dad – may he rest in peace – died before y'all got famous, but I always think he would have loved you. When *your* dad died, I asked my dad to bring him into heaven with a big ol' hug. Felt so bad for you young gals. Are you getting the band back together? You know we talk about you all the time. And those magazines, they stopped printing those stories about y'all, and that's a good thing, but we never believed a word they said anyway. How's the little one? Lana?"

The back of Adele's throat itched. "Fine." She had no idea how Lana was since she never answered Adele's phone calls. The ache of it was dull and familiar. "Do you mind if I have a look around? While I wait for Nate?"

"Sure, sure." Norma bobbed up and down behind the bar, spinning into action. Tomato juice, sliced celery, vodka. "A Bloody Mary doesn't just appear out of nowhere. Gotta work at it." She frowned and looked upward again. "Unless you stare into the mirror, you know? And say those words? I'm not gonna do *that*. Okay. There." She added a dash of Tabasco. "Mine isn't as good as Nate's, but I'm getting there. Just gotta keep working on it."

Adele wandered towards the rear of the saloon. It was just as she remembered it, dark and dusty, smelling of splintered wood and spilled beer. The old jukebox glowed neon blue and green in the far right corner. Next to it was a skinny ATM that had been added since she was last here. To the left of that ran the long bar all the way to the back wall. How many buckets of ice had Adele hauled out of the old storeroom? The girls had loved being there in the saloon, still under-age, helping Uncle Hugh with stocking and refilling in the afternoons. They'd begged to be allowed to stay as late as they could, listening to the music, not leaving until Sheriff Tate came in after his shift and raised his eyebrows at the little girls doing their homework in the far left corner on the big, scarred wooden table.

The table was still there. Adele touched the top of it, feeling the ridges with her fingertips. People still carved their initials into it, using penknives and ballpoint pens. They didn't cut deeply (out of respect, perhaps – surely they would have dug more deeply into a tree) and the well-worn initials looped over each other, years and years of couples who had loved and lost and loved again. When Adele and her sisters had done their math homework here, they'd had to make sure their notepads were under their papers, or their pencils would stab through into the table's scars.

Somewhere on the table were their initials, too. All three of them, *AD + MD + LD. Adele and Molly and Lana.* Hidden now somewhere, buried by the map of other letters.

Adele realized she was humming and closed her throat. She heard the refrain of "You'll Never Leave" in her mind. Then she wandered back towards the front door. To the right was the stage. Just a couple of feet higher than the floor, it was made of the same old wood and, if she remembered right, just as rickety. Impulsively, she jumped up onto it, stretching her arms wide. A light snapped on above her head, and she grinned in delight. Even when they were kids, Uncle Hugh had kept that motion-activated light there, and they'd loved the way it had shone down on them like a spotlight.

"Sing us a song!" called Norma from the other side of the saloon.

Oh, hell, no. Adele swallowed her grin and raised a hand. "Maybe later." Or maybe never.

The old pool table stood in the same spot it always had. Adele could imagine a tsunami sweeping in and taking out the Golden Spike, carrying away the saloon and the café and the old hotel – the whole town of Darling Bay itself – but that pool table, as heavy as sin and older than Eve's apple, would stay right there, right where it had always been meant to sit. At some point over the years, the felt playing top had been repaired. Chalks, the old square kind, were lined up on the rail, and a half-dozen cue sticks leaned drunkenly against the short inner wall.

Adele could almost hear the crack of the balls. Molly had been their ringer, always willing to bat her eyes innocently at whatever guy thought it would be fun to show off his pool prowess to teenage girls. Molly would run the table, stick the guy's money in her pocket, and then ask Uncle Hugh for a round of root beer floats for her and her sisters.

Molly. She wanted Molly here.

She pulled out her cell phone. *Remember the root beer floats?*

Holding her phone in her hand in case the text actually managed to soar out to the cruise ship somewhere on the ocean, Adele used her other hand to lift up the bench seat in the front window alcove. There they were, all the board games they'd spent so much time with. She'd be willing to bet that the Monopoly set was still missing all the Get Out of Jail Free cards. (Sheriff Tate had gotten his feelings hurt one night when he'd been on a particularly expensive Monopoly losing streak.) And the Sorry! game . . . She pulled it out and lifted the lid. Yep, there they were. Each piece had little teeth marks at the top, marching all the way around. The blue piece was missing the round knobby top altogether.

While Adele raced around the board, passing her sisters with a cheery "Sorry!" Lana would get so mad she'd chew the pieces, leaving her tooth marks behind, or in the case of the blue one, biting the top right off.

Adele glanced left. Norma was looking into her Bloody Mary as if it were telling a fortune, so Adele quietly slipped the headless blue piece into her jeans pocket. From the layers of dust inside the bench seat, no one would miss the piece anytime soon.

She looked out the side alcove window. Across the middle parking lot stood the old café. Funny, she'd assumed it would still be open, that Hugh's employees would still be running it. But it was shuttered and dark, an unbearable sense of loneliness coming from the ripped awning. She looked right, up to the slight rise behind the saloon and café. That was the hotel, the third old building that she'd called home every summer of her youth. It was where she would sleep tonight. She yearned for that, for this already-long day to speed up until she could just lie down, close her eyes, and breathe in the ocean-scented air.

The phone – the real one that hung on the bar's back wall – jangled. Adele jumped. Norma grabbed it without hesitation. "Golden Spike, this is Norma!"

There was a pause. "Yeah." She grinned. "Right again. You bet. I'll keep 'er running, boss. Yeah. Okay. And hey? I forgot to tell you I need a raise." She slammed the phone down with a hoot of laughter. "That was him!" She looked at Adele as if suddenly surprised to see her. "Oh! I should have told him you were here."

"No, that's okay. I'll see him when he gets here."

"So I guess *you're* the boss around here now." Norma was obviously startled by the thought, her grey eyebrows shooting higher. "Of course you are. Oooh." Her drink wrapped tightly in her hand, she leaned forward from her bar stool. "You should tell him to hire me. I wouldn't drink all the booze, I *swear* I wouldn't." But there was a twinkle behind her expression that said the opposite was true, and that they both knew it.

CHAPTER 29

Nate shouldn't have answered his cell phone that morning, but he was a sucker for a blonde. Especially if the blonde happened to be ninety-one and living on the boat he'd sold her five months earlier. Ruthann Suthers had asked, "Does it matter, dear, if my extension cord in the kitchen smokes a little?" Nate thought of the electrical fire at the hotel, and told her to call 911. She said, "I already did. They said it was okay, but they shut off my power." Nate had sighed and spent the next two hours crawling around the baseboards in the boat's mess. He'd installed three new surge protectors, and he'd tested each outlet. By the time he'd finished, he'd bruised a knuckle and ripped his favorite Merle Haggard T-shirt.

And he was late.

At least Norma had been at the bar to open up. Unless a wandering tourist or two showed up, she'd probably be the only customer until three, anyway.

He parked his truck in front of the post office. Getting out, he pulled his Charlie's Feed and Seed ball cap on backward. What he really needed was another shower.

Maybe he could bribe Norma with a couple more drinks off her tab to stay a little longer while he cleaned up. He took the two shallow steps up off street level with one long jump.

Inside the saloon it was dim compared to the bright morning sunlight. Norma grinned at him from her regular bar stool. "Boss!"

"You keeping out the riffraff?" Too late, he noticed that someone else *was* in the saloon, way over by the bench full of board games. "Whoops." Not even a tourist – a pretty tourist, at that – wanted to be called riffraff.

"Nah, they're getting in. And hey, guess who it is."

He looked again. The woman was standing straighter now, pretending not to hear them. She kept her eyes out the side alcove window as if there was something more than just the old, closed Golden Spike Café across the parking lot to look at. And she wasn't just pretty. From this angle, she was a sight closer to beautiful. God, who did she remind him of? She must have driven up from the city or something. Some model, waiting for her photographer to shoot her on the beach. He'd seen it plenty of times before, pretty girls thinking it would be good to get shots of themselves in the water, or leaning against the high cliffs down at Fenton's Cove, not realizing that the fog bank usually made it not only a shoot in bad light, but also a shoot where they'd freeze their dang nipples off. If they stayed till October, maybe. That's when the sun came out around here, after the summer tourists had given up all hope and left. But this woman, with her honeyed hair and that perfect long nose, those lips that were quirking into something that looked like it was close to a smile, she'd be shivering in her two-piece soon enough.

"Howdy," he said politely. If his ball cap had been

forward-facing, he would have touched the brim, but as it was he left his arms at his sides.

She turned to face him, and in that motion his heart dropped to the old floorboards and went right through, straight down to the dust and packed earth below, not stopping until it hit the world's molten core.

Adele Darling. Out of freaking *nowhere*.

CLICK HERE TO **keep reading *The Darling Songbirds***

Firefighters are hot, sure, but so are dudes who can do construction. Men who can build *and* have a reality show? You don't want to miss these hotties!

KEEP READING for a preview of the first book in The Ballard Brothers of Darling Bay series, ***On The Market***.

ON THE MARKET CHAPTER 1

Felicia Turbinado put her rental car into park and glanced back down at the address she'd scribbled on a Post-it. The numbers she'd written matched those on the side of the purple house, yes. So this must be it.

But she'd expected an office-looking building.

This was a dark purple Victorian. And it wasn't a stunning architectural marvel, nothing like the Painted Ladies of San Francisco hours south of here. This place had peeling paint and warped glass in the windows. The small, attached garage seemed to be listing away from the house itself, as if it were trying to slink away without being noticed. The steps that led up to the front door had been dark blue at one point, but footsteps had worn the paint off in the middle of the stair treads. A wind chime hanging from an eave just clunked, its strings tangled.

The sign in front read *Ballard Brothers Building and Realty,* though. It had to be right.

Felicia checked her bag. Contract and deal memo, yes. Signing pen, yep. Non-disclosure agreement, check. Sometimes she carried bribes from her boss with her—Apple watches in 18-Karat gold cases or floor-level season tickets to the closest national basketball team.

But Natasha said this guy was perfect for the new show, and more than that, he wasn't the kind to even know to ask for a bribe. *But just in case, take the big American Express.* Felicia patted the side of her purse as if to reassure herself that with that amount of credit, she could get almost anything done.

Natasha trusted her to close this deal. The brothers would agree to buy a house for a single woman chosen by the network, and then they'd remodel it on camera. Hopefully, attraction would spark between the female buyer and one of the brothers (and the network was willing to pay as much as it took to make that happen).

This was important. Felicia checked her lipstick—the deep red was on her lips and not on her teeth—and her eyeliner was smudged as artfully as she could manage. She got out of the car and gave a sharp tug to her red blouse. This might be a sleepy beach town that smelled of salt and sunscreen, but she was no surfing tourist.

She walked past the rusty old truck in the driveway and went up the stairs. She gave a quick rap at the door.

"It's unlocked, come on in!" The bellow was accompanied by a crash.

Felicia swung the door open.

"I'm in here, to the right!"

The floor was old and dark, and the air smelled of ancient wood polish. To the left was a small office with a cluttered desk that stood in front of windows open to the street.

"Keep going—I'm in the kitchen!"

"Hello?" She peered around a doorjamb.

"Hey there!" The man's back was to her. His hair was short and dark, business-like, and his neck was wide. He turned his head briefly and she caught a glimpse of a broad smile, white teeth. His hands moved rapidly, juggling bread bags and at least three different kinds of jellies. "I just gotta get these sandwiches done."

The house might be old, but inside, it looked classically remodeled. Everything looked vintage and in perfect condition. The refrigerator was lemon-colored. The stove was light orange. A cheerful blond wooden island matched the beveled cabinets. The sheer height of the far windows was astonishing—they let in the view of a massive rear garden. From where Felicia stood in place, her bag pressed to her side, she could see a tangle of tomatoes that looked ready to take over the nearby beanstalks. A long picnic table stood on a low deck, surrounded by heavy outdoor chairs. It looked like a perfect place to hang out. Or to serve a million peanut butter sandwiches, although didn't they have a meeting scheduled? "I'm sorry, did I get the time of our meeting right?"

"Yep, yep, I'm just running a little late, that's all. Let me slap some lids on these bad boys, and we'll get down to business."

"Can I help?" The request was automatic. He'd turn her down, and then they'd have their meeting. She could talk him into the terms of the show, answer all his questions, get his and his brothers' signatures, and be ready to shoot as soon as they found a woman who wanted to buy and remodel a house with these guys.

"Really? Sure. Those all need their crusts cut off. These seven are fine, but Timbo's allergic to peanut butter, so I have to make sure I make his almond butter and strawberry with different utensils. No cross contamination, you know?" He turned to face her.

His eyes were astonishing—a bright, very light blue. Robert Redford eyes. The color of calving icebergs. He had to be wearing contacts. Didn't he? He wore a blue button-down shirt and a darker blue tie, beautifully tied. His shave was smooth, his chest was broad, and his wrists were wide. He looked like a realtor, and a successful one, which is why it didn't make any sense at all that he was working on a production line of sandwiches.

"Felicia, right? I'm Liam. Sorry my hands are too nut-buttery to shake."

"Of course." Smoothly, Felicia swallowed her surprise and set her purse down on the kitchen table. She washed her hands at the sink, and then picked up the knife. "This is more jelly than I've seen since the grade school cafeteria."

"I swear this won't take long. I'm almost done."

Felicia cut off an edge, and then another. It was too bad she hadn't come with a camera crew. How perfect was this? "This was the way I wanted my sandwiches cut when I was a kid."

"I always liked the crusts best myself."

"My mom said that's where the nutrition was."

"Well, no wonder you didn't want to eat them. Nutrition is fine. But not fun."

Felicia liked his voice—it was deep, with a ragged edge. He sounded cheerful, as if he laughed a lot. Maybe he'd actually be likable, a welcome thought. Scouting trips for the network were usually deadly dull—there was a lot of time spent talking with people who had stars in their eyes and no real knowledge about how television worked. They thought that talking to a network rep meant they were guaranteed fame, fortune, and a line of housewares at Target.

Felicia had met with women who got plastic surgery just to talk to her. One woman had barely been able to smile around her newly-full lips (they hadn't ended up signing her). There was talented and there was camera-ready, and often they didn't go together.

"Do you live here, too?" It didn't seem like an office kitchen—it seemed like a place a person could cook a holiday turkey or make blueberry pancakes.

"Yep." He glanced at the ceiling. "Upstairs. Okay, I need about six more, then we'll be good."

"Who are we making these for? Do you run an orphanage?" *Please say yes.* Damn, she *should* have brought Tony. Her cameraman would have done a slow pan on the old-fashioned kitchen and then a tight zoom in on Liam's wide hands scraping out the last of the peanut butter. Start the story with his adoration of the children who surrounded him, end with him being in love? The network hadn't managed an Emmy yet, but that might do it.

"You could call it that," he said. "Okay if we deliver these on our way? Won't take long, then we can scout houses. I have a few properties that might work."

"Sure." Heck, yes, she wanted to watch this man deliver sandwiches to whatever lucky group was getting them.

The network might swing and miss at random shows, but Felicia's boss Natasha was rarely wrong. She'd come up with the whole idea while on vacation in the small town of Darling Bay, and it didn't look like she'd be wrong now. With this guy on a show? People would tune in. And the more people who tuned in, the bigger Felicia's bonus would be. Maybe this sleepy little seaside burb would turn out to be all right. No matter what, it had to be better than the show Felicia had just wrapped about a group of sisters trying to break into the soap-making world. If she never had to smell boiling lye again, it'd be too soon.

A NorCal beach town in summer had to be better.

And even though Felicia vastly preferred watching on-screen talent from either the edit room or the comfort of her own sofa at home, it wouldn't be difficult to work with this man with the melting icecap eyes.

Liam should have expected that the network producer would be pretty. Even though Darling Bay was ten hours north of Los Angeles up the rugged northern California coast, and even though Liam hadn't had cable in years, he knew enough about Hollywood to know that no one was ugly in Tinseltown.

And this woman was stunning. Even in high heels, most women couldn't meet Liam's eyes straight on, but she could, and Liam stood an easy six two. Her dark brown hair was thick and long and curled—it hung to the tops of her breasts, which were round and high and probably fake. She filled out her red shirt perfectly. Her legs were miles long in tapered black pants, and her black heels had to be four inches high. Spikes. Who wore spiked heels in Darling Bay? Cowboy boots and flip flops were the two most popular footwear choices in town, always had been.

He opened his car door. Might as well get this half-baked idea over with so he could get back to the rest of his day. "Here we go. Sorry, I was driving a buyer around yesterday, and I don't think she broke five feet. Just shoot the seat back, that button there."

Felicia nodded and settled into the passenger seat with a long stretch, smooth and graceful. The leather seats gave a sigh like they were happy to meet her.

"Is that okay? You comfy?"

She smiled. "Perfectly."

"Good. Good." His throat felt tight.

Felicia made him nervous.

And that didn't set right with Liam. Yet one more thing that rubbed him wrong about this whole idea.

But he'd be polite about it. If it didn't work, it wasn't a big deal. He'd tell her he couldn't help her. It happened, after all, every once in a while. He'd agree to take a potential client to look at open houses, and on their first trip out, it would be obvious they couldn't work together. The person would be too aggressive or too impatient. Liam liked making money, sure, but he already made enough day to day. He didn't have to take on clients who would be problems from start to finish.

And being on a reality show? Liam's brother Aidan had said it was a stupid idea, but his youngest brother Jake had laughed and called it too weird *not* to look at closer. Liam had been drunk when the idea had come up, and didn't *quite* remember why he'd agreed. So this was on him, really. He'd finish out the meeting with Felicia, show her a couple of houses and prove to her that Darling Bay wasn't the small town they were looking for, and then he'd shake hands politely and vamoose. He'd send a polite email saying thanks but no thanks, that they just didn't have the time. He should have already done that, but this woman's boss, Natasha, had been pushy when she called, and telling a woman she couldn't have what she wanted was his least favorite part of being a realtor.

But the money.

Damn it, with the money Natasha had implied might be in it for them, he and his brothers could start the after-school program for at-risk youth they'd been trying to talk the city into creating for years. They wouldn't have to wait for the city council to agree, they could just do it.

Felicia spoke as if she were interviewing him on camera. "So what makes you good at your job?"

Liam turned right on First Street and gave a quick wave at Vivian Engel. "Never really thought about it."

"You must have."

"Dunno. I guess I just like to make people happy." After-school program or no after-school program, TV didn't make anyone happy. Liam's gut was right—he knew it. He'd be polite, show her around, and then wave her off into her Hollywood sunset.

Felicia shifted slightly in her seat so that her body faced him more. He caught the scent of her perfume, thick and sweet and rich, like jasmine on a hot night. "Tell me more."

"It's not a big thing. I just know what people are looking for." Aidan called it Liam's superpower. *Me and Jake get 'em all riled up but you calm 'em down, so we almost cancel each other out.* "I can figure out what buyers want before they're really able to verbalize it. And then I just show them those properties."

"So you already know what I'm looking for?"

Her voice was business-like, but it held a sultriness that could earn a woman like her lots of free drinks in dive bars. Nah, on second thought, a woman like Felicia went to intimate, cutting-edge clubs where you had to use a password to get in. She'd probably never set foot in a restaurant with peanut shells on the floor or a bar that smelled like spilled beer.

He pushed the button to roll down the window, suddenly too hot. "Sure I do."

"Tell me." She rolled down her window, too.

Warm summer heat filled the car, and Liam regretted not blasting the air conditioning instead. "Big. Light. Airy. Open plan kitchen, a long redwood deck that overlooks the ocean. Marble and granite floors. Loft bedroom." He glanced sideways at her.

Was that a grimace? "You'd think that, wouldn't you?"

"What?"

"Natasha explained her idea to you, right?"

Liam thumped the gear shaft into second as the pickup in front of him hit its brakes. "Yeah. Sure. Um, did she happen to mention that I was drunk as a skunk that night me and my brothers met her?"

A cool nod. "She did."

"That was only like a month ago. Y'all move this fast?"

"Always."

"I have to say, I *don't* really remember her goal with all this. Some kind of TV show, I know, but Aidan and Jake and me, we're not sure why the hell anyone would want to watch something in a little whistle-stop town like Darling Bay."

"People are tired of glitter." She pointed at Martha's Market. "They want charming. Small town. Warm. Do you know who those people are?"

In front of the store, Parrot Freddy stood with a bird on either shoulder, talking animatedly to Dot Rillo. Freddy had been up in arms since the price of postage stamps went up last summer, and even though Dot only worked at the post office and didn't set the postal rate, Freddy brought it up with her every time he saw her. Dot usually just took the opportunity to try to get Ethel to squawk her classic, *Polly's an idiot, give me a Twinkie.*

"Yeah, I know them."

"See?" Felicia clapped her hands together quickly. "That's what we want. Small-town *The Bachelor* meets *The Property Brothers*, only there are three of you, so that's even better."

"Yeah. Those property guys are kind of creepy, don't you think?"

"Really?" She sounded astonished. "They're handsome twins. People love them."

"They're so *manicured.*" If that's what they were looking for, the Ballard brothers would be right out. Aidan only shaved once a week, maybe twice, and Jake lived on a boat, for cripe's sake. "And they're *actual* twins. It's not like we're triplets or something. We're not that interesting."

"You're Irish triplets, right?"

"Is that even a real thing?" Liam pulled into the driveway at the south end of the high school.

"You're each separated by ten months, right? Like Irish twins?"

"Ten and a half." If you wanted to get technical.

"Your parents were busy."

Yep. That's what everyone said. Predictable as summer fog. "They were also missing in action by the time I was five."

"You're *kidding.*"

He glanced at her as he pulled up the parking brake. Had those bright green eyes of hers actually lit up at the thought of them being essentially orphaned?

Television people, man.

"This'll just take a second. You wanna come with me?"

She smiled. "Yes."

That *smile* of hers. That was the kind of smile that launched a thousand ships, or at least the dreams of them. For a reckless moment, Liam imagined saying yes to whatever this woman wanted. "Come on, then."

The man was a dream. He was everything they'd been looking for. And this was supposedly the non-rugged one? How could that *be*?

They walked along the edge of the parking lot and passed a swimming pool that was surrounded by chain link. Liam's stride was long, and Felicia had to take quick steps to keep up. Blasted heels. What had she been thinking, putting on Louboutins? This wasn't Rodeo Drive, and she knew it.

They passed an empty tennis court, the ground pocked and uneven. The whole school had a run-down vibe, the paint worn off and faded. Seagulls argued at the edge of a dented trash can and pulled at something that looked like a potato chip bag. Graffiti on the handball wall poked out from under a haphazard application of green paint.

This was *so* not Beverly Hills. The show would want a shabby-chic seaside vibe, but not in a Coney-Island-in-winter way. Hopefully they wouldn't need footage here.

Liam stopped in front of the basketball courts. "This is it."

Once Felicia had gone to the Cinque Terra in Italy to scout a possible vacation reality show. The idea had ended up tanking, and she couldn't even remember the premise for it, but she'd never forgotten the old man she'd met at the water's edge in Vernazza. He'd been impressively short, dressed in an old blue suit. He'd chattered at them about his loves, all of them. *I've had so many loves in my life. And look, here are a few of them.* He'd opened a bag and started setting down kibble right onto the pavement. Dozens of cats —who had been invisible until that moment—appeared from every direction. They ran at him, mewing and crying, and Felicia thought she'd never seen anything sweeter. An old man, surrounded by fifty-plus cats, all of whom loved him (or at least who had loved his treats).

The boys on the basketball court reacted to Liam the same way. Two balls that had been in play bounced by themselves to a stop as they crowded him. The kids seemed to come out of nowhere, more of them every time she looked.

"Quick!" He handed her a heavy paper bag. "Crustless, these ones here. One goes to Timbo—"

"Me!" A boy tall enough to be a man with a face too juvenile to allow him to buy cigarettes raised his hand. He leaped at the sandwich she held out in its plastic bag. "I'll take two! No, can I have three?"

Liam gave her a quick nod. "Jones and Logan get crustless, too."

Quick hands shot out and relieved her of her burden.

"Who else? Jimmy, you like grape, right?"

"Thanks, Liam!"

"Thanks, lady!"

"This is Felicia, say hello…"

But as quickly as they'd arrived, the boys were gone, all

of them chewing and jumping and leaping, taking huge bites while simultaneously throwing the retrieved balls at the backboards. Even the cats in Vernazza had taken longer to finish their dinners.

"Okay, that's taken care of."

"Is one of those kids yours?"

Liam balled up his paper bag and shot it at the trash can, making it easily. His fist pumped. "Two points! You ready?"

Felicia blinked. Liam was easy on the eyes, all right. He'd be great in front of the camera. His smile was wide, his teeth white and straight. Even though he was ostensibly the paper-pusher of the brothers, it was obvious that his blue button-down shirt hid a muscular chest and a flat stomach.

She needed to stop staring. "Yeah."

Back in the car, Liam was more talkative, as if the brief visit with the boys had relaxed him a bit. She hadn't noticed he was nervous—and most regular people were, talking to networks reps—but he must have been.

Now, though, he'd loosened his tie a notch. His elbow stuck out the open window as he narrated their drive. "Down there is the main fire station. See, where the flagpole is? They're about to do their boot drive, and that'll be fun."

"Boot drive?"

"Once a year, they stand at every intersection in town holding a uniform boot, and people throw money at them. For every balled-up dollar bill that lands in the boot, they have to do a quick dance."

"Is that a punishment for something?"

"You kidding? Those guys love to show off. Two of them know how to break dance. They put those guys at the stoplight."

"*The* stoplight? Singular?"

"We just need one."

"Wow." Felicia did a calculation in her head. "When does this happen?"

Liam's smile faded a little. "Why? You want to get that on camera or something?"

"I have to tell you, Darling Bay seems almost too good to be true. We want stories, and everything you say seems to be the start of a good one."

"Well." Liam turned his head, and Felicia couldn't see his expression. "Let me show you the properties I had in mind before you get too excited."

"I don't get too excited."

"Oh, really?" He sounded amused.

"Unflappable." She wouldn't admit that she was feeling more hopeful than she normally did on scouting trip.

"Is that as fun as it sounds?"

"Less," she admitted.

KEEP READING!

Keep reading by grabbing *On the Market* now! Just go to RachaelHerronBooks.com to get your copy!

(Psst - there are special discounts over there, too!)

ABOUT RACHAEL

Rachael Herron is the internationally bestselling author of more than twenty books, including thriller (under R.H. Herron), mainstream fiction, romance, memoir, and nonfiction about writing. She received her MFA in writing from Mills College, Oakland, and she teaches writing extension workshops at both UC Berkeley and Stanford. She's a New Zealand citizen as well as an American.

She'd *love* to hear from you! Sign up for her mailing list at RachaelHerron.com/Subscribe, then drop her a line and she'll write you back! (Seriously. She loves to hear from readers.) Plus you'll get a free short love story that will melt your heart, instantly! Or find her on social media!

instagram.com/rachaelherron

patreon.com/rachael

facebook.com/Rachael.Herron.Author

bookbub.com/authors/rachael-herron

youtube.com/@RachaelHerronWrites

www.ingramcontent.com/pod-product-compliance
Lightning Source LLC
Chambersburg PA
CBHW061438210726
48287CB00007B/2262